living
with the
dead

Philip G Reed

The Book Guild Ltd

First published in Great Britain in 2019 by
The Book Guild Ltd
9 Priory Business Park
Wistow Road, Kibworth
Leicestershire, LE8 0RX
Freephone: 0800 999 2982
www.bookguild.co.uk
Email: info@bookguild.co.uk
Twitter: @bookguild

Copyright © 2020 Philip G Reed

The right of Philip G Reed to be identified as the author of this
work has been asserted by him in accordance with the
Copyright, Design and Patents Act 1988.

All rights reserved. No part of this publication may be
reproduced, transmitted, or stored in a retrieval system, in any form or by any means,
without permission in writing from the publisher, nor be otherwise circulated in
any form of binding or cover other than that in which it is published and without
a similar condition being imposed on the subsequent purchaser.

This work is entirely fictitious and bears no resemblance to any persons living or dead.

Typeset in 12pt Adobe Jenson Pro

Printed and bound by CPI Group (UK) Ltd, Croydon, CR0 4YY

ISBN 978 1913208 271

British Library Cataloguing in Publication Data.
A catalogue record for this book is available from the British Library.

For Nish, Jem and Chloe

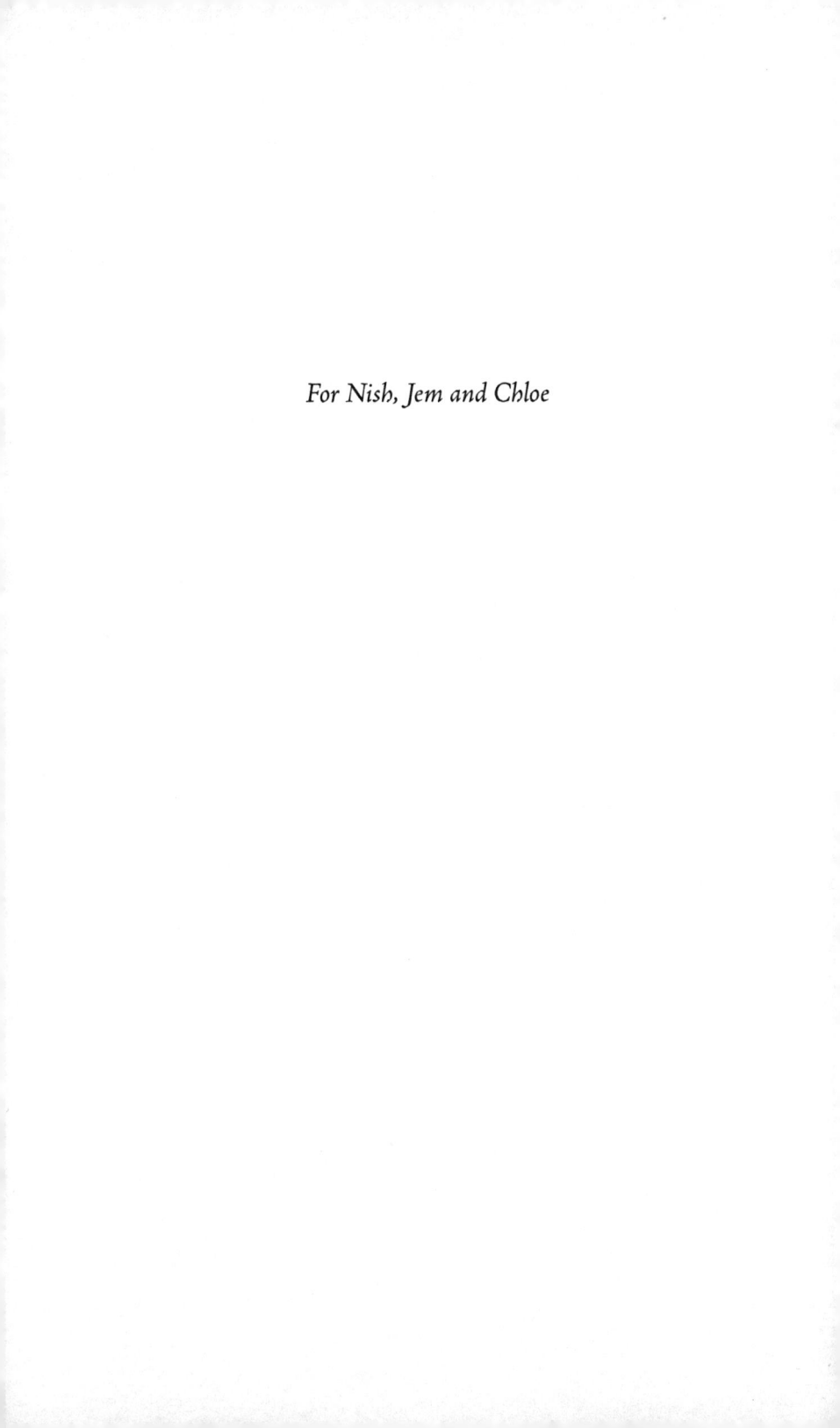

prologue

Rebecca

Devon, 1935

"You might not be a man, but make people forget that and you could succeed at this game."

That was how Sir Robby had started my training. But now I'm not playing anymore and, man or no, I'm having this bastard's brains out. Iron-shod bucket to the temple and he'll be down, and down for good, but I can't see through these damn tears. Got to hit him. Kill him. He's there by the barn and I'm running, swinging it hard.

But I'm stopped, held fast, I can't move, get off me, I twist and wrench, but strong hands pull me back and I hear screaming and my throat is burning and the man is crying; why is he crying? He did it. He killed him. He killed him. But my strength fails in the farmer's arms and I'm falling, limp to the wet yard, held and screaming.

I say, "Let me go," sobbing through a lump that I know will never leave me. "Let me go, he has to pay."

My Robert.

Magsie

2010

I LAY TWO MORE LOGS IN THE GRATE. I'M RUNNING low on oak. I'll have to start using the fruitwood from the old apple trees that Simon took down years ago. It won't burn as long. All the same, I'll feel better about burning that, somehow, than the oak, which could have been put to some better use than warming up an old woman. One of the logs falls through the hole I melted in the grate once, burning coal. Silly sod. This end of the village always was the coldest. Hard ice. Frosted panes. A chill that gets into your bones. The cold rolls down the hill and fills up the hollow where my house sits. Up to the eaves. I never minded the cold before, but I mind it now.

 I stand up from the fire, slowly, my hand on the irons to steady me. I reach for the mantel, rest a moment. The warmth of the fire hard against my legs and softer as it drifts up to my face. I turn away, still a grip on the mantel until I have my free hand well towards the arm of my chair, lean into the movement and swing round until I can drop down onto the cushions. Simon propped up the wooden feet a few years ago so the seat wouldn't be quite so far away, but it still always feels a long way to drop. I give myself another moment.

I can't see all the pictures behind me from here, but I can feel them. George graduating. George at school. George with his new bike and his socks pulled up at the gate. George's paintings.

The arms of my chair are brown and shiny by now. I ought to get some covers for them. I run my thumb over a seam. Should I have some tea? I don't want it. But… sit here for a few more minutes and, up, again. All my weight, such as is left of it, on the arms of the chair. I feel my knees taking the load and I set off across the room. The kitchen's all still tidy, all still neat, but it doesn't seem to bother me anymore that the plate has a slightly greasy feel, just a little, under my thumb-tip. It's OK. It's only me now. I have a little cheese and a little bread. Nothing strong-tasting, nothing complicated, and some tea. Just a cup.

I squeeze the bag against the edge of the cup and brown clouds into the water. I see Simon's face as I do it, grimacing and moaning about strong tea giving him a dry mouth. I fish out the bag. The bin has a long handle I can pull to open it. I never did get on with the pedal and now it would be a non-starter. I'd probably fall over.

The bag makes a splat onto Tony Blair smiling up from the semi-darkness with his crooked teeth. A disappointment, that man. The polling station had been too far last time and I hadn't booked my postal vote, so this was as much disapproval of him as I'd ever been able to register. Still, better than nothing.

I turn up the television so I can hear it across the room. That Andrea Rippon is telling someone off for not knowing something or other about some tennis player or other. Is it

Andrea or Angela? Is it even Rippon? John McEnroe, though, I remember him. I wonder how old he is now. Grey-haired, probably. Probably still making longer journeys than across the room, though. But he'll get there, if he's lucky. Or maybe if he's not.

I click off the Andrea-or-Angela woman and the house is quiet again, apart from a lorry passing and what I think is someone washing a car on the other side of the road. Simon used to wash the car, oh, once a year at best. Always grimy. Surprising, really. I think that was his only lazy streak. Otherwise, he was spruce and smart. So was the house. And the garden. Vegetables when we were younger, raised beds with flowers when we were older and gardening had to be gentler. My dad's car was the same. Funny, now I think about it. Although Dad's was always clean when we had the visitor. Now when must that have been... far, far back. Before Simon and I were married, that's for sure. Simon wasn't long arrived down in the country from London and he wasn't best pleased at this other new chappy being even more glamorous and exotic than he was. What was his name? Something foreign-sounding. He worked hard, that one. And then all that story came out. My goodness.

I wake up bleary. What's this room? I can't lift my head for a moment. Slowly, slowly, I can see around. Carpet, chair legs, wall, doorway, kitchen. Ah, yes. I know. Been sleeping in my chair again. George behind me again now. And Simon, dear Simon. Hassan must be dead now, too. Only me left out of everyone that lives in those old memories.

Hassan, of course. That was his name. He came and stayed for a year... two? Working in different places in the village. Stayed in a few different places, too, but mostly with us. The other chap came along too, a little later. And that poor woman.

A sad one, she was. But I smile when I remember the look on my dad's face when he came bursting through the door with his shotgun.

He arrived at the end of the summer in, oh, when would it be? I take a breath in and blow it out. Between the wars, anyway. And Simon was there, fled out from London for the green trees and spaces and the clean air and the quiet and the cool. We were married in 1935. I remember that one. Now there was a year.

Rebecca

India, 1932

OH, DRAT IT. HOW CAN THEY SEND SUCH A LITTLE tender to pick us up? Madness in this sea with the wind blowing us all about! But here it is, crawling over the water like some broken old spider, and the only way to get to land. My jaw tightens up again with nausea as the bright blue water rears up and falls away, but I tell my stomach that we'll have no more of its silly nonsense and make to climb down into the boat.

This part of the coast – from what I can see of it as we're paddled into shore with the men's oars slapping and splashing around hopelessly – looks as I've been led to expect by more seasoned travellers to India, mostly during the weeks long sea voyage to Bombay, before this shorter trip north. The stone path and some walls here and there at the quay are the most robust looking man-made things around. Mostly it's wood and seems to have been built in a hurry, carelessly. Wooden houses, wooden carts, wooden boats pulled up on a scrubby beach a few hundred yards away. As well as the salt smell of the sea, there's a hint of fish, old rope and tar drifting to us over the water. I urge the men on, using my best coxswain's voice from Oxford. "That's the ticket, get us in, chaps!"

This is where I've come to be with the dead, and with him, and landfall can't come soon enough.

The others follow as, at last, I lead the way from the water, my legs finding themselves again on the too-solid ground. Now then, where's this excavation? We've had quite enough time in a ship-bound hiatus of tedium and vomit, and now I want to get cracking. India and a real archaeological dig. I'm out of stuffy England at last and, what feels almost better, out of my own time and into another.

I pull at the new close-tailored trousers that cling to my legs in the sweaty heat. It took a lifetime to find any that weren't enormous flag-like things as most women seem to wear these days, but now I wish I'd followed the fashion for once. But thank heaven that my hair is in its usual bun; it would have been simply awful to arrive with it all blowing around like some silly woman's. What on earth would the men have thought? I check it again to make sure it's tight and march the few hundred yards to the shade of a sorry-looking palisade, flapping all the while at Robert to keep up. "Come along, old boy," I say, "my freckles are burning. Anyone would think you didn't want to be here."

He shrugs and says, "Funny, that." Then, with a – perhaps forgivable in the circumstances – touch of irritation, "Where are they all anyway? They must be around here somewhere."

No-one else speaks, but a chap sitting near to us and making – well, I'm not sure what – something rather complicated out of some sticks and string, points towards a canvas awning a short distance further inland. I can just make out that people are moving sluggishly around beneath it, as if struggling under the lead-weight of the midday temperature. Not much vim around here.

Although, now I think about it, didn't we hear that the sun almost killed someone on-site a short while before? Baked out in the field, like some unfortunate plant from my mother's house, taken out of cool grey air to somewhere hot and dry and left to wilt. Yes, that's right, the man had only recently arrived from England and bolted off almost straight back again. Seems a bit of a poor show, that; isn't a bit of roughing it what you come to these climes for? It would be jolly rum if you toiled all the way over the sea and it looked like Ealing. And anyway, we'll be better off than him, although I do feel a trifle pink in the skin already and, if I'm quite honest, a little green otherwise.

At the awning, I step into the shade, such as it is – the canvas really offers hardly any protection – and drop my creakingly new leather satchel onto a trestle table. With a flutter of nerves, I realise that beyond it is a large encampment: the dig, at last! It's all a little ramshackle and threadbare, and I imagine that if they tried to relocate the various tents and canopies now, they would crack like so many wafers. But generally, a splendid, wild, Percy Fawcett-type of business, it looks like to me. Although, let's hope it's not too much like one of his shows; I'd rather not disappear into the jungle, never to be seen again, like dear old P.F. did in '25.

Seeing us enter, a man whom I take to be Colonel Ashton comes across and interrupts my musings by offering water. He shakes hands with Robert, murmuring, "Lieutenant Baker," and looks me over slowly, before offering only a rather clipped, "Miss Hellings."

Ashton's leading the dig here, and it's quite something to be before him at last, this man I've read so much about in the weeks while I was kicking my heels, waiting to set off. He's brought to the practice of archaeology a new and rigorous method; his excavations in Mesopotamia were a *tour de force* in earthy precision and now it's India's turn – jolly well try and stop him. I wonder how such a man will welcome me – a female ignoramus – into his habitat, and I can't say I'm enormously encouraged as he describes to Robert the last few weeks of work. It's more complicated than one might have thought and a bit of a deuce to follow. Still, I knuckle down to do my best, so I'm a little cross when I find after a few minutes that I've somehow tuned out the Colonel's voice, like turning the dial on the wireless, and become wholly absorbed by Robert, by what an admirable fellow he is, what a dash he cuts, standing still and easy, one hand in a trouser pocket in the pose I've seen in so many London pubs, while Ashton jitters about as if his body's trying to keep pace with a mind that's leaping between aeons of time: earliest man, the dawn of civilisation, the great Bronze Age traders. I mentally tell Robert off for being so distracting and refocus just as he asks Ashton about the men on site.

"We do our best with the Indians," answers Ashton. "Dig hard-ish. Not that well. Not punctual. In the end we set them up in tents here so they couldn't fail to be at work on time. Natives, d'you see, of any sort, can't be relied upon. But on the upside, you can drive 'em, hard as you like. Natives don't mind it. None of your rights or unions here, thank God." His speech comes in sharp bursts, in a voice that's hard, with the edge of command from his military days, I suppose. After this little summary of the Indian contribution he grunts, seeming pleased with himself.

"Well, we'll do our best to keep up the British end," I cut in, keen to move him on from a subject that's making me a little uncomfortable and threatening to cloud over my excitement.

Ashton turns to me: "Now then... Yes. Miss Hellings. How's your Uncle Peter?" and, with a blacker look, "Don't make me regret the favour I've done him in having you here."

Before I can respond (a little hotly), a small voice comes from back amongst the tables and charts in the shelter: "Hellings? You must be from Devon." A woman in glasses has straightened up from working on a large map and I'm about to reply, but Ashton rides over me cavalry-style, proclaiming, "Well, never mind all that now. To the trenches, I think!"

He marches off towards the excavation, with us scurrying behind. The great dig is some few hundred yards from the main encampment, which he seems to have set up in deliberate isolation. Ashton says, though, that he drops in on the site unexpectedly from time to time to keep the workers on their toes. "Don't let them feel too cosy. They need a tickle now and again." I must say, cosiness of any sort seems jolly far-fetched; just look at this place: the wildness of India, the men with their dark skins and tough bodies, the bright leaves, the white sun, the dust. And everywhere, the immense weight of foliage that seems fit to burst with life that yowls and shrieks and chatters.

After a brief tour, we're dismissed and, little knowing what to do for the moment, troop back to the awning. There, our friend in the glasses sees Robert and me standing about rather hopelessly, and after watching us for a moment or two, comes to our rescue. She ushers us back into the shade and summons fresh water from the well and some food. In the heat and dust, I wonder briefly how on earth she keeps her brunette ringlets so neat and fresh-looking, not to mention her crisp white blouse, pushed up to the elbows. Well, however she does it, it would be too much trouble for me. With another appraising look at both of us, she takes off her spectacles and wipes them carefully with a lace-trimmed handkerchief drawn from a pressed cuff.

"Don't mind the Colonel," she says, "there's been a dry spell in finds and he gets a bit… fractious. He's quite the little boy, wanting a present." She hops about on the spot, aping him perfectly: "Demmed natives, demmed hot, demmed food, demmed dust, and no treasure!" Robert and I both laugh like drains at that. Dropping Ashton as quickly as she took him up, she goes on, "He's desperate for a big discovery. In all seriousness, it's not much fun at the moment, the place is feeling pretty charged, I can tell you." She touches my arm. "I'm actually rather glad you've turned up," then, turning to Robert, "both of you."

For my part, I thank heaven that here we've found some youth and spirit to help us rub along out here. She's off again at breakneck speed, now about the excavation itself. I begin to feel even less qualified to be here as she goes on, "Ashton's worked through tons and tons of detritus from recent occupation – you were lucky to miss that – and he really got his tail up" – I don't know why, but I blush a little at that – "when he got down to some burials about eight feet down." She dons Ashton again, like a suit: "Buried 'em there for only a few hundred years. Wasn't a settlement for long. You can tell by the demmed artefact chronology," a brief aside to me, "and please God, Miss Hellings, try to avoid a lecture on that," before she resumes as the Colonel, "it's a New Culture I've found. A whole New Culture, I say." She pronounces the capital letters quite perfectly.

I interrupt her show, feeling that I should perhaps try to learn something as well as enjoying myself. "What does a New Culture mean? It sounds a little grand. Is it simply hot air?"

She pushes her spectacles back up her nose, her face turning more serious as she realises, I think, that I'm actually interested in the archaeological side of things as well as her. "Ah, well," she says, "it's not quite as over the top as it might sound. The thing is, these bronze cremation urns we're finding – that's what they put the ashes and bones in – have a little decorative device at the shoulder, where the neck joins the rounded body." She shapes it in the air with her hands. "No-one's ever seen anything like it before. It's… well, it's quite remarkable. And honestly, to give the old chap his due, it's an important discovery."

"A device?" I venture.

"Yes," she goes on, "it's a face, actually. A sort of a death-head. It's all to do with what dying meant to these people, the way they treated it, the symbolism." She seems no longer to be looking at us directly, but inward, seeing the images in her mind's eye and, perhaps, imagining the ends of all the lives that went to fill up all those little pots.

I'm itching to ask more, but Ashton steps back under the awning and, evidently having overheard the last few moments of description, starts sketching out one of the faces in the earth with the handle of a riding crop. He holds the whip end with his fingertips, gingerly, as if it were hot. I wonder at that for a moment but forget it as he almost skips about, telling the story of the great finds. By this point I'm getting pretty keen to see these urns for myself, all of which have apparently been removed to a strong cabin that Ashton has erected for their safe storage; I ask if we might have a viewing.

We make our way there shortly afterwards and, in the semi-darkness of lamplight and strips of bright hot sun striking through the wooden slats, I gently run my fingers over the warm skull faces, my skin prickling at this contact with the deep past. But all the same, I do think that declaring a whole new 'culture' of people based on some pots seems, well, a bit much. But, then, what do I know? And surely it *is* curious that these things are found nowhere else, despite the fact that apparently Bronze Age trade routes here covered hundreds, if not thousands, of miles to Europe and even the Far East. Why should these burials be so isolated? And why had the cemetery been so short-lived – what happened to these people? Despite my slight scepticism, it seems to me that if Ashton can uncover the story of these ancient faces, this site could be enough to found books and fame on, maybe even a lasting legacy for the old warrior.

After that, though, Ashton bustles off again and Robert too, evidently not satisfied by the small spiced pasties we were given earlier, strolls off in search of heartier food. But I'm loath to leave these beautiful objects in the half-light amid the smell of hot wood and dust. I imagine the other hands that held them in pain and grief all that time ago. Suddenly, I recall my neat companion: "I'm so sorry, I haven't even introduced myself," I say, holding out my hand. "I'm Rebecca. Hellings. And yes, you're quite right; I am from Devon."

Magsie

SIMON WAS GOOD IN THE GARDEN. SOMEHOW, HE just had a knack. I used to love it, but I wasn't what you'd call able. But I needed it – really needed it – when Simon died.

Rough grass, dry leaves, cold autumn air and woodsmoke. I had to feel myself in the world like that, be within all its smells and textures. Holly, ivy, pink blossom, peeling cracked woody stems. Wood grain and soil under my fingertips.

Strong hands I had, back then. Younger, soft skin that would dry out over a morning's work, to be refreshed at lunch with one cream or another. People brought so many lotions and things. They thought they'd help me. I don't know why. Though it was better than the flowers, I suppose. I had too many flowers; it made me think of the funeral all over again.

I used to enjoy my hands turning from soft to hard and dry, like green roots growing out into the land, turning brown-grey and gnarled. It felt like my fingers joining with the earth, turning into it, like Simon was doing. And all those others. All those others.

I'd push my fingers into the earth, feeling my edges seem to blur even as my skin hardened. I can remember the stumpy grass under my knees, the rolling of the lawn amongst the raised beds. Mowing for the first time of the year on a March day, with the air too cold for that real cut-grass smell. That earth out there kept me going for so many years, like all the others that have lived in this house. Lived and died in this house, I'm sure. How many potatoes, how many carrots, from my old garden? Four hundred years of them, that's for sure. Maybe more.

My mind's wandering. I should go to bed. Hassan was a good gardener too. He knew how to lift a crop of potatoes. Didn't lift too many seasons' worth of them, mind, but he had the knack. No bruises, no spuds stuck on tines.

I get up again. Slow, slow. Take my time turning round the arm of the chair and through to the hall into my bedroom. I turn on the tap to wash and spin it closed, squeezing the last turn. I always enjoy that. Satisfying, squeezing off the water. Take my teeth out. Drop in a tablet to fizz away gently. Fizz away the day. Bubbles rushing up in silence, their little pops too faint for my old ears to hear. I drink a glass of water and suddenly I can see the room more clearly again, as if the lights have been turned up a bit brighter. Things look real again. I've been letting myself get too dry.

I reach out for the bed, push the sheets back, lean down, and turn and drop my bum onto the mattress. One leg up. The other up. Put my head down. There. I wriggle my feet in the cool, clean sheets. My body presses into them only lightly. There's not as much of me as there used to be.

Well, I slept then; for a long time and Simon was there. You beautiful man. You silly old fool.

You were jealous of old Hassan, I remember. How old was I then? Only a girl, really, a slip. Always following him around, I was, and didn't really know that I'd already turned Simon's head. I wouldn't have turned that Hassan's head, though, not that one. Simon wouldn't have known there wasn't any danger. I laugh aloud and the sound booms in my quiet room. The walls aren't used to it.

"Ah, well. Another day and still alive. There's a nice surprise," I say to no-one but the house. I slide my legs across the bed, put one foot down, and the other foot. I've got this handle I can hold on to and the bed's high, so it's not too bad. Up, slowly, slowly, hold on. I'm up. I rest a moment, feel my body calming down again after the effort, and move to the sink. Now, let's have some teeth.

That boy turned up here out of the blue, looking for someone. What was the name of that one, now? A local name, was it? I run my hand down the gloss-painted doorframe. I don't know, I can't remember, but Hassan just turned up and said he was looking. It was the old farmhouse where he came, when it was my mum and dad's house. The village was smaller in those days. Not that I've seen the old place for a long time. We didn't go there much after we moved up the country.

Dad's own farm, it was. Not much there any more, I heard. The farmhouse is, but no-one's living in it. I expect it will be pulled down one day. I remember Dad saying he really did pull down one of the old farm cottages once – with a tractor and a chain round the chimney. It must have been a rickety old thing. I'd come down with a chain round my chimney these days. Maybe not a bad way to go. It'd be quick.

I'm dry again, want some tea. I walk into the living room, past my chair, hold onto the shiny arm, and through into the kitchen. There's still the crockery from my sandwich there... well, never mind, the girl will come later. Time was I'd never have let a visitor in with dirty crocks out, but there you go, that's what happens. Standards go. Hassan used to love tea, he liked me to make it, loose leaves and a pot. Just a Tetley bag now.

Ah, I used to laugh with him. Perfect English, he had. Well, more or less. "Will you put me some tea, Magsie." It was never a question. He knew what he wanted, that one. He wasn't scared, either, even though there were some that weren't so welcoming. I suppose he'd seen a lot. Most of the villagers had never met a man from Persia before; probably none of them had, now I think about it.

He'd normally say 'please' if I raised an eyebrow at him, though. I was good with my eyebrows.

He was almost happy for a while, I think. But not in the end.

Rebecca

'Yes, Devon, of course. I caught your surname, didn't I?" she says, introducing herself as Erica Conston. "I recognised it from our church – in St Adestel. There are a couple of 'Hellings' plaques inside. I think there's a vault, too," and, with a slightly mischievous smile, "well-to-do family, is it?"

I laugh. "Not at all! If the roots of the family were rich, none of it came up our branch. You grew up in Devon, did you?"

"Yes. Yes, and I'll be back there again soon, I think. I'm chiefly doing my own research here, really. The dig gives me pocket money to survive, but once I've got enough material, I'll be off back to England to write up my findings."

India, she tells me, has been Erica's home for a few months. She had heard of Ashton's dig through an old army colleague of his who is attached to the British administration in Aden, and whom Erica had encountered during a break from ethnographic travels, while she was taking stock and editing a lengthy manuscript she'd worked up while on the road.

"You must be so busy," I say.

"I am." She rubs the sides of her head with her fingertips. "Too busy. I'm enjoying it but… well, speaking plainly, I really want to get out of here. I like being an anthropologist, but I was always more of a university library girl than very much into fieldwork. It's simply exhausting. And Mother, well, she's agitating for me to get married. Thinks this academic life and being among," she coughs slightly, "people who aren't… well, British… is all very improper. She's rather old-fashioned, I'm afraid." She keeps rubbing away at her head before seeming to come to herself again. "Anyway, Rebecca, you don't need to know all this."

"It's all right," I say, waving my hands awkwardly, and, with an inward grimace at how gauche I must sound, go on, "I was hoping we could…" more hand-flapping, "be… friends. You can… tell me your troubles if I can tell you mine." *Please, do let's be friends*, I think, and Erica reaches over and gives my arm a squeeze and immediately, I know we shall be. I beam at her and change the subject: "Do you think it odd that he has two women working here? It must be unusual."

"And two young women at that," says Erica. "Or young in your case, at least. I'm a bit… worn out." She pulls her cheeks into jowls and I laugh, protesting that she's being unfair. "But yes," she continues, "I do wonder why. I mean, good on us for getting out in the world. There are lots, I mean thousands, of women who'll never have a chance like this. But I don't think his motive is to broaden the modern female mind."

I laugh again. "I wonder why my uncle is such good friends with him. I suppose he might have been different back in his college days, when he was young." I ponder for a moment. "He might even have been a bit handsome."

Erica makes a sour face. "Let's not get carried away, Rebecca."

Feeling by this point that I've probably had enough of my own awkwardness and, indeed, archaeology for a first day, I decide to see a bit more of the people who are actually still alive around here. And anyway, I don't feel quite ready yet to start settling into my lodgings. We're to stay with local families and the introduction to my hosts is inevitably going to be terribly uncomfortable. Frankly, I'm dreading the whole arrangement. I'd have been happier with a tent if I had it to myself. Well, a comfortable tent, anyway. With a bed.

So, I make my excuses to Erica and walk back to the village. There are a few men by the shore, fresh from the water with a huge silvery catch of mackerel. The boats are decorated in faded colourful paint with steep prows, and the slick and shining bodies – some still moving – are heaped within. I ask, as well as I can, for some fish and am sent with much good-natured gesturing to some shabby buildings above the high tideline where earlier catches are being prepared in sauce over a small fire. I hand over a few worn coins and settle on the shimmering sand.

Beyond the beach, the forest begins. Or perhaps jungle would be a better word. Now that I look at it, I'm astonished at the brightness of the green, the flowers of so many colours and shapes that you can see even from a distance. And the burble, squeak, cry and rustle of who knows what creatures living their lives out of sight. Fanning myself with a large, veined leaf, I scoop some of the hot food with something I think they called a *roti*. The hot fish in its bright-red juices is like nothing I've ever tasted before; I'm a little startled by it at first but eat greedily, with the sounds of the majestic, wild place all around me. This will do.

Magsie

I don't see George much anymore. Scotland's so far. Or my little granddaughter. And I don't suppose he'll have any more now. Although it's never too late for a man. He'd need a new wife, though, and I wouldn't want that.

He doesn't visit any more than once a year, so how many more times will that be? George was born in this house; you'd think he might want to come back sometimes. I miss him. And my little Elspeth.

Stop that. Too much thinking sad thoughts. It's not good for a person. Maybe I should go outside. But it's raining now. I'll try it anyway. I must feel the autumn air. Never know when it might be my last chance, and I've been too closed up. It's only a few steps from the kitchen to the front door. Come on, Magsie Brown.

I grip the door handle. Hard to push down and turn at the same time. I feel the bones in my arm moving, turning against each other. Now it's open and the cold, damp air rushes in at my face. It's wonderful. Probably not good for me, but what does that matter?

I take a step outside, holding tight to the handle of my stick and hoping its rubber end doesn't slip on the wet ground, where it's worn and the bottom flaps as it's coming away. The stone's wet and gritty under my slipper. Another step and I reach forward for the gate and turn towards the garden. Cold water runs through my hair and trickles into my eyes. I can feel it soaking through the shoulders of my nightie. But this feels good.

Old pots still out by the garage, no proper plants in them anymore, bits of grass, some weeds. Tiny round green leaves in some, like pebbles. I find the big old pot that someone got for Simon and me when we'd been married – oh – thirty years or something. He stacked it up on bricks so he could still reach it to weed when he'd stiffened up with his back. I grip the rim. Rough under my palm. An old, stiff hand now, but I can still feel the textures. I put my hand onto the little green pebbly leaves, push through them into the earth. Soft and wet mud. I move my hand around a little. The gutter's been running into the pot a bit and it's got sloppy. I try to wipe some of the mud off my hand on the edge of the pot. Some of it flicks onto my wet nightie. Bugger.

Maybe I should sit down a bit. The surge of energy I had when I came out and felt the air is fading fast. I'm getting cold. I lean on the wall. The gutter's running down over my hand where I'm still holding the edge of the pot. But I should dig out these green bits while I'm here. Tidy it up a bit. I scrape them away and throw them down onto the concrete path. Still more in there. I scoop up another handful and lean on the edge of the pot with my other hand. Getting tired. The pot moves on its bricks, overbalanced. One of the bricks has slid out, like in the big Jenga thing the children play in the park. The pot's on the edge now. If I let go, it will fall.

"Bugger it. Silly sod," I say out loud. Breathe. "I'll just get this out." I reach in again with my free hand for some more of the little weeds. A gust of wind flicks the gutter water across, soaking into the other side of my nightie. The pot moves again. My hand's starting to hurt where I'm holding it from falling. I take a moment. Assess things. I can let the pot go. It will break. That will be sad. But I don't have the strength to hold it. I'll need to step out of its way, so it doesn't hit my legs or my feet. But I don't know if I can. I can see my pale old leg breaking in my mind's eye where the heavy pot cracks into it. *That's going to hurt... What if I...* I try to lean on the pot, can I push it back onto the steady bricks? It's too heavy. It won't move. Where would it be best to drop it? Try to get it to hit my foot? Or my shin? If it hits my shin, it will probably hit my foot anyway. So let's go for the foot. Part of me is still thinking calmly, working out options, and the other part is screaming at me, "You bloody old idiot! What the bloody hell are you doing out here in the rain?"

My face is wet, but I can't tell if I'm crying now or if it's the rain. My breath is getting ragged. Can't reach my stick. It's fallen from where I leant it on the wall.

Where's Simon?

Rebecca

THE NEXT DAY, WHAT SEEMS TO BE CAUSING A FEVER in Ashton's mind even more than the face-urns is a lighter-than-usual shade of mud. I'm definitely going to need some more persuading before I can get very thrilled about that, particularly after the horrid struggle I had to sleep in the heat last night.

But my mood lifts after some hot frothy tea made with milk fresh from the cow and some fruit, only slightly bruised and dusty, and we're told to get ready for a trip to a new part of the excavation site. I've dressed in another pair of my linen trousers with a clean white close-fitting blouse. I think this will be something of a uniform while I'm here and, after all, there's little need to dress up. I've also put on my trusted leather boots again, that have seen me up mountains in the Lakes, through Yorkshire dales, and around the fields at home. Most recently, they took me on a route through the South Downs (with a man who, in the end, didn't work out) and here, now, is a bit of the Sussex earth still clinging to my sole and carried all the way to India. I smooth my hair back and put my satchel, with notebook and pencils, over my shoulder. Yes, it does feel so good to wake up and start the day here. I even forgive Ashton for a lingering look he runs over my figure as we set off.

When we arrive at the site, I see that the men have cleared the topsoil from a large area that at first looks just to be a uniform brown square. Ashton excitedly pours a watering can with a very fine rose onto the light dusty earth and urges the diggers to do the same all around him with more cans, until the whole area is dampened. The Colonel's can sloshes as he puts it down, and with that and the sight of the water sparkling in the sun all around, the heat of the day seems to bear down all the more, and I pull out a canteen for a drink.

Robert sidles up. "You going to share, old girl?"

I drink on a little longer, playing that I'll finish the bottle. He narrows his eyes at me.

"You minx," he says in a low voice and, gripping my arm, "I might have to throw you into this trench here." I let out a little shriek and all the men look round. Even Ashton glances over, frowning slightly, before continuing with his lecturing. At last, I hand over the bottle, its cool metal neck still moist from my lips and watch Robert drink, see the liquid spill from his mouth and onto his shirt-front, where it dries in moments.

Looking back, I see that the sprinkling of water from the cans has brought out contrasting tones in the soil – a long, lighter-coloured strip of earth has appeared across the centre of the trench. Ashton, skipping on the spot, jabbers on. It seems that this light patch is in fact the trace of a very ancient, very long, very special monument. But somehow, again, all I can see is Robert; the curve of his neck as he drinks again, his slim arm, brown already in the sun not like my silly pink self, the way his shirt is pressed just so, the sharp line of his parting and the beads of sweat on his fine brow.

I turn away. Don't be silly, Rebecca, let's keep our sights a little lower. There'll be plenty of good, honest chaps out here and you can snag one of those, if you must. What was it Mrs Bruce used to say at school? "Girls, in life you need to aim for realistic, rational, rewards. Play safe and you'll not get hurt." Perhaps there was some wisdom in that, even if she was only urging us all to be typists.

All the same, I never could put Robert out of my head as easily as that. And Ashton calling him 'Baker' as he calls him over to point something out drags back an old memory, from long before we'd ever thought of coming to India. It was after a long and boozy dinner one winter at the Savoy as the piano played, that Robert told me he had hated his family name while at school. "Not because of the family. Because I'm not a baker, damn it. The rotters would say I'd come from the shop, ask for some bread rolls, order some cakes. It really stinks, being treated like that when one's young."

I remember him picking up his scotch glass and raising it to his lips but dropping his hand back down to the table with a thump, the smoky scent of the spirit drifting up when it splashed onto the white cloth and polished silver. He was quiet for a while, then told me that there had been other things too; mostly the ribbings hadn't really been about the name. The boys had seen something in him that others hadn't, something they didn't quite like. He hadn't fitted in. I'd been surprised about that at first. Robert had always seemed a bit of a swell to me and I thought he'd have always been popular. Well, not quite a swell, maybe, but I'd been sure he would at least have made friends easily enough.

He had his moments of, I don't know, awkwardness, I suppose. The odd time when you weren't sure what he was thinking or what he might do next. When he seemed to be speaking to you from somewhere else. Like that night at the Savoy, when he stopped speaking and gazed across the room, the candles, quiet diners and sumptuousness, and seemed to have entirely forgotten I was there, the scotch drying on his hand. But nothing in him had suggested to me a boy who'd been a misfit. Once he'd told me about it, I felt that we became closer but, then, perhaps he didn't feel quite the same. Oh, I don't know.

Maybe I can say no more than his school days hadn't been happy, and that, for me, means a bit of kinship at least. I didn't have a terribly hard time, but a girl who, though quiet, wears trousers and otherwise acts fairly like a chap will tend to find herself being a little singled out. I had very few friends growing up and I carry that knowledge with me even now that my school days are fading. Not that I went into all that self-pitying nonsense on that particular evening, though, being all too eager to change the subject on to where on the Strand we might go next that would still be serving drinks. Robert wasn't quite so keen to leave the topic, though, I remember.

"It was that whole place. The whole county. All those dreadful little market towns."

"You don't go back?" I said.

"No. I won't. There's no point. There's nothing I'd want to go back for. What's not actually offensive is… well, boring. Everyone's so… small."

I looked at him and cracked with laughter. It was one of those laughs that simply wouldn't stop, growing even as I tried to stifle it. I bent double in my seat with my face nearly touching the table and tears starting from my eyes.

"All right, all right, old girl. I mean small-minded. You know what I mean."

I calmed down. Caught my breath. "Sorry, Robert," I said, "you don't have any family still down there?"

"No, not any more. My parents have been gone…" he waved a hand vaguely, "for years now. There are probably loads of cousins and God knows who else still about but, really, who cares?" He leaned back in his chair, stretching with his fingers laced behind his head. Then, on a long breath out, and much too loudly for the room, he said, "Oh, damn them all to Hell."

He smiled and I blushed as all the other diners turned their heads.

"You don't have much family either, do you?" he asked once they'd resumed their meals.

"Well. Not many people, I suppose. But we're all very close."

Robert grunted, and said, "So you're lucky in that anyway."

I wasn't sure which part of my comment he meant.

I remember him walking me home that night, miles across London. I said we should take a cab but there weren't any around – or at least any that would take us south after midnight – and anyway, despite the distance I think Robert wanted to feel the air, the cold prickling of mist against his face. To spend a bit more time out in the wide world before the night was done. He had his hat pulled down low, I remember, against the cold, and a red scarf wound round his neck and down his back. He took my arm.

When it started to rain, he held his brolly over both of us, but it was a narrow, flimsy affair and we'd each ended up with one wet arm.

"You're giving me the cold shoulder," I admonished him, and snatched away the umbrella, leaving him laughing as the rain poured from the brim of his hat.

I suspect that the watering can lecture will be only our first encounter with Ashton's long pale 'monument' and his theories on it and, for today at least, what with the distraction of Robert, my skin prickling in the sun and my eyes stinging where sweat trickles down from my brow, I really can't process it much. Ashton, having drawn Robert aside, is droning on to him, and a number of English students and other acolytes are hanging around to speak to the great man when they have their chance and, I think, maybe to get a bit closer to Robert, the new and beautiful addition to the scenery. Time for me to slip away from the crowd and recharge. The high wind of the previous day has dropped, leaving the air still and stifling. My clothes seem to claw at me; I need to get cool.

Wishing to pass the village unnoticed, I walk quickly through an area of dusty woodland, the shade of the trees like a balm on my skin. I spare hardly a thought for any snakes or other creatures that might be lurking as I march along, and my feet are quickly covered over in fine, ash-like powder. I reach a steep bank, covered with thick bushes, at what I think is maybe half a mile south of the village and the fishermen's beach. If I can just find a private stretch of shore, I can swim.

The thought of cold saltwater makes me quicken my pace down the bank, and about halfway down I slip and slide the final portion on my bottom. Now, quite covered in dust, I push my way through another curtain of undergrowth and onto pebbles that give way to sand. I stop and catch my breath, listening for anyone who might be around. All is silent, except for the sea rustling at the shore and a solitary bird calling out a tune over and over with an increasingly frantic air until, all at once, he stops. I've come to a small bay, protected by a rocky headland to the north, which obscures the village entirely, being covered in trees clinging to its surface with tenacious roots.

To the south, the land is much lower, and a long spit of sand arcs out and away. Here is my chance. In almost a fever of anxiety to get out of the heat and dust and into the water, I half-unbutton my blouse and pull it over my head, unlace and kick off my boots, and pull off my trousers.

The sea is glorious, warmer than I'd expected but deeply refreshing after the breathless heat of dry land. It glitters dazzlingly and I can barely open my eyes when looking out to the waves on the deeper ocean. After wading out to shoulder depth, I turn back to shore, seeing my clothes and boots scattered where I left them, reminding me of my near-nakedness, here in the water, the sea exploring every part of my body, washing away all the last traces of dry old England and baptising me into India. I close my eyes and sink under the surface, feeling my hair spread as I pull out my bun. I let myself float for a while, drifting on my back, the heat from the sun on my chest and face. With my head half-submerged as I float, the world is silenced but for my heart beating and the sounds of the water and I let a harmless, hopeless fantasy of Robert play out in my mind's eye; he and I here in the water and all our clothes back there on the sand.

I lie like this for what feels like only a few minutes, then lift my head and drop my feet back towards the sandy bottom. Goodness, I've drifted out. The beach is a narrow white stripe, far away. Swallowing down a moment of dread at the vastness and depth of the sea behind me, I kick for land.

As the sand comes up to meet me from below, I stop swimming and start to walk again, the odd pebble finding my toes as I make my slow way. I wonder where Robert and Erica are, whether they're still being subjected to Ashton's lecture. Robert doesn't know what he's missing out here. There's a little burst of excitement in my chest as I picture bringing him here to swim – even for a more chaste outing than the one I've been imagining – but the feeling vanishes when a movement near the tree line catches my eye.

I drop quickly back down, only my head above the surface. Is there someone there? Thank God I kept my underwear on. Keeping my eye on the trees, I move sideways towards the headland and slip behind a large rock. I watch and wait, and as I do, the stupidity of what I've done begins to dawn on me. This is India, not Kent. I'm not swimming a few yards from ha-penny arcades and candyfloss stalls. There could be any kind of wild animal lurking there out of sight, waiting for me. I cling to my rock, while the sun moves westward past its zenith. I was looking for privacy not an hour ago, but now I hope beyond anything to see people again. To see Robert. Anyone. Are there tigers here? I strain to see, for my eyes to penetrate the thick foliage and reveal whatever is watching. But did I really see a movement? Or did I dream it?

After another few minutes I know I have to do something. I can't stay here in the water any longer. It would be too far to swim round the headland and, anyway, going beyond it would mean getting into deep and open water, and to risk either being swept onto the rocks or out to sea. No, I have to get home by land and no-one's going to help me do it. Slowly, inch by inch, I creep around the rock and make my way towards the shore. I keep my eyes fixed on the spot where I think I saw the movement. Once on the beach, I move quickly to where I dropped my clothes, ready to dash back into the sea at any moment. I pull on my blouse, yanking it desperately when it sticks for a moment, covering my eyes. There's a distinct crash from the trees and my heart lurches in my chest. I stare about for some sort of weapon and in panic pick up a stone the size of a cricket ball. The foliage stirs again and there's the sound of heavy, padding feet. I ready the stone in my hand. A hard throw between the eyes and even a tiger might be stunned, giving me a chance to run for it. The leaves ahead of me part and I make to throw.

"Rebecca. Good Lord, what are you doing here? And why aren't you wearing any trousers?"

"Erica." I let the stone drop from my hand onto the beach and nearly sob with relief, the vision of a tiger with a lump on its head tearing me to pieces receding from my mind.

"You've found my bathing spot," she says. "Good swim? Did you think…"

"My God. I thought you were some beast of the forest looking for lunch. Didn't even think of it until I was in the water. Is it dangerous? I mean, are there snakes and… things?" I don't want to mention my fear of the tiger yet in case I sound quite ridiculous.

She laughs, touches my arm with her fingertips and thinks for a moment, her forehead furrows slightly. "Well, yes, I wouldn't really recommend solo trips; I always bring along a guard when I want a swim. You're right, there is wildlife and so on that you must be careful of here, snakes and so forth, you do need to watch out for those. But there's…" She trails off.

She turns and calls to someone still lurking amongst the trees, "Harpreet, come and say hello. Rebecca, this is Harpreet Kaur."

A small but strong-looking woman, quite without teeth and whom I take to be about fifty, steps forward. She has a machete at her hip and holds a long, rusting gun that looks a hundred years old. She bobs her head at me. Her jaw is set tight and small, a collapsed mouth puckered above it, her expression otherwise entirely blank.

"I keep Harpreet with me when I'm alone, because it's not only the animals you need to be watchful of. There are all sorts of people around here, Rebecca. Harpreet's nephew, Amar, told me that he's seen a man recently, in the forest. Armed. He didn't know who he was but said that he looked, well, not… usual. He might be dangerous."

"Heavens, Erica. Now I do feel silly for wandering off alone."

"And I'm afraid it's worse than that," she says. "A few days ago a child went missing."

"Oh, how awful. And do you think…?"

"We don't know," continues Erica, "but… well, it looks that way. It happened once before, Amar said, many years ago. A lost sort of a man appeared near the village. People got a little used to him after a while but were always wary. Then one day, he was gone and a little girl was gone with him."

"Oh, Erica… how simply—"

"Yes. It's frightful. It could have been anything, of course, a cobra, anything at all really, in this place. But it seems that the child's mother never had any doubt."

Harpreet steps past us now further towards the sea and looks back along the line of trees and undergrowth where they meet the sand. Erica holds my eye, and silently dips her head towards Harpreet. "It was her little daughter, so you can imagine that she's pretty agitated now that it seems to have happened to someone else, too."

"Oh, good heavens," I say quietly. But I feel it best to change the subject. "Is it… quite usual to have a female bodyguard?"

"Well, I should think it is, for swimming," says Erica. "You wouldn't want a man hanging around would you, with nothing to do but watch?"

At that, she strips off to a dark blue, high-throated swimming costume, a white ribbon in a bow at the waist.

"Are you coming in again?"

"No, I think I've had enough for now," I say, my skin feeling tight and salty where it's dried in the sun. "But you carry on. I'll sit here for a while."

This seems such a darling place to look at, I think, as Erica swims back and forth, keeping her ringlets above the water. But I can't shake the thought of that poor child. I must make enquiries about it. And be a little more cautious myself. But now, I'm tired, and as Harpreet continues her patrol, I stretch out on the sand and soon drift into sleep.

As I fall away from the brightly coloured world with its furnace air, Robert comes before my eyes. I'm in the water, struggling with something, a serpent or a kraken. I can't see it, but it clings all about me, snaring my limbs and twisting me under the water. Robert's trying to help, pulling at the winding sinews that grip at my face. I feel my throat closing. I can't breathe. But slowly I realise it's Robert who is trapped. Black coils crushing his chest. His arms twisted impossibly and his mouth opened in a silent black round as his face turns inwards and he is lost. I scream for him, but no breath comes.

When Erica returns from the water, I start from my sleep, gasping, looking wildly about me. The terror slowly slinks away.

Erica touches my arm, laughing. "Bad dream?"

"Gosh. Yes. Sorry." I rub my face vigorously. "So silly."

She must have read more in my face than I'd have cared to let on, as her eyes shine with mischief as she says, "Dreaming about anyone I know?"

"No," I say. "No, nothing like that. Oh dear." I desperately will my face to turn any colour other than beetroot. "It was about… there was a monster, it was sort of clawing about and dragging me under the water."

Erica clearly doesn't believe it for a second. "Oh, well," she says. "If you had any other dreams, ones that you might… want to come true some time… well, you never know what might happen out here. We're a long way from home, you know. If you ever want me to, well, help something move along a little, let me know."

How can she just address it outright like that? The front of it, how can she be so forward? And more to the point, how could she even know? Heavens, she mustn't say a thing to Robert. She must not. Panicking, I bluster something about not knowing what she means, while she smiles an infuriatingly knowing smile and shakes her head. "Fine, Rebecca," she says. "Don't think I'll give up that easily, but if you'd rather stick to work for now, I can fill you in on what happened after you scurried off..." She thinks for a moment. "Now, Ashton said that this 'monument' thing, as he calls it, is a long man-made mound. He's had the men dig down right through it at one point, and that's been enough to get him very excited. He was even saying that you could tell what it must have looked like when newly built – merely from reading the earth – and that it would never have been very high, so it can't have been for defensive purposes. It's something entirely symbolic, he's sure. Maybe magical," she added, raising her eyebrows at me. "Apparently in the early morning, you can see where it runs across the landscape, if the sun catches it in the right way, something to do with the grass growing taller where the ground's been disturbed or... well there's some clever theory about it, anyway. But the most interesting thing about it is that it's so long – Ashton's dug the trenches out to forty yards or more but can't find any ends. His big idea is that the thing's curved and actually circles round one of the foothills a little inland from the dig site. If that's right, it would be, well, vast, one of the biggest Bronze Age monuments ever found. Anywhere."

I'm relieved to see that Erica has actually managed to divert herself fully from her speculations about Robert and me, as she's assumed that serious face she has when discussing the archaeology, but I become less pleased as she goes on. "But he's dug it all so quickly. The men are... He shouldn't drive them like that." I realise she's turned a little pale beneath her tan. I start to ask her what's wrong, but she cuts me off with a slight shake of her head, and after a moment continues with her explanation.

The line of the mound, she says, corresponds with a shallow ditch on one side, around twelve yards wide. That ditch is long since filled in with plant growth, wind-blown sand and the detritus of hundreds of years so similarly is nigh on invisible, except to the trained eye. It seems the long mound was built from the spoil of the ditch and must have been quite precisely wrought. Ashton supposes it must have been faced with vegetation, or wood, or something else now perished, to keep its form. All this he can tell from a secondary trench some few yards away, cutting a section through…

But this is all getting quite exhausting, even to listen to. "He does get very excited by all the little details, doesn't he?" I say. "What does it mean, does he think? Isn't it a little queer to spend so much time asking 'what' without asking 'why'?"

"Well, perhaps. But they're sort of the same question," says Erica. "If they went to the trouble to build it all terribly precisely and to try to preserve it, maybe that tells you something about what it meant."

"Oh, well… I suppose so."

"And Ashton actually thinks it does *mean* something quite extraordinary," she says. "He's not sure what, yet. Well, not exactly. But he thinks it must have something to do with treasure or something." She's got that worried look again now. "Look, the thing about Ashton is that he thinks he's the great scientist but really… he's not after mere knowledge – it's not for the good of Mankind." One of those capitals again. "He wants the hoard of gold, the secret tomb of the murdered child-prince, the battlefield of shining warriors or some such grandiose thing." She pauses. "What he really wants is fame."

She's chopping the air with her hand now and getting heated as she goes on. "Think of the thousands and thousands of hours of crippling work that must have gone into that mound and he's only really interested, only really thinks it's worth anything at all, if it can lead him closer to building his own monument. He's really a damned hypocrite."

Her anger spent for the present, we sit quietly for a moment. The sun is passing over the headland now and its long shadow creeps towards us over the bay, the air cooling as it comes on. The light seems to have taken on a thick golden quality and to ooze and cling about us, unwilling to be driven out by the advance of evening. It's still hot, but I shuffle a little closer to Erica on the sand, where we sit side by side. "Quite the atmosphere here sometimes, isn't there?" I say.

Erica nods. "Maybe that's why the Bronze Age crowd hung about and got so inspired too." I start to say that I meant the iffy atmosphere on the dig itself, but let it go. Then she turns fully and looks at me closely again. "But what brought you out here? Shouldn't you be doing something a bit more..." She waves her hand, seeking a word.

"Boring?" I suggest, laughing. "I've tried, don't worry. I was meant to be safely at work in London by now, but I don't know, I wanted to get out into the world for a while."

"At work?" she says. "Well, that's not altogether conventional either."

"Well, it is really. I'm not as exciting as you might think."

She punches me gently in the arm. "Don't do yourself down," and flopping back onto the sand, "God, I'm glad you're here, though. That man, Ashton, I know I'm droning on about it, but, well, this week's thing is to plot out the course of the mound using stakes and he's got the men rushing about all over the hillside in the middle of the day, in this heat. The poor dears can barely keep upright once he's done with them for the day." She lapses seamlessly back into her mimicry. "Had to lay those out to show the Indians what they were supposed to be digging. They quite fail to understand what we're doing. 'Why should one piece of earth be any better than another, unless for farming?' No point explaining; simply keep paying them and keep food in their bellies. That's all the Indian understands. Natives don't have the capacity."

Erica pauses and shuffles a little more on the warm sand. "Look." She purses her lips, then continues, "I'm sorry, it's not fair to get into all this when you've just arrived. But he doesn't think the men are really people at all, rather that they're some sort of lower species." I grimace, fearing this is true. For a few moments, Erica looks like she's steeling herself to say something. I'm beginning to wonder what it might be when she finally says, quietly and looking down, scraping her feet back and forth making small trenches of her own in the sand, "And Mr Baker, too. Does he think that way?"

I look at her, a little shocked. But she goes on, "When the Colonel was talking about the diggers, I thought I heard Mr Baker say something about 'savages' to one of the students. I didn't catch all of it, but it sounded like… well, it wasn't complimentary."

"Robert?" I say. "Surely you must have misheard."

"Oh, maybe. Probably, yes," she says. "Ashton was booming on and I couldn't hear very well. I thought I should say, because…" She pauses.

"Because what?" I say, trying to fight the flush that I feel rising up from my neck again.

"Well, I thought you should know, that's all," she finishes, and waves her hands in a placatory way. "I'd rather know, if it were me."

Surely Robert wouldn't have been so awful. It's the 1930s, for goodness' sake. He can't be harbouring those sorts of

Victorian attitudes. He's only really in India on sufferance, of course, and because I put a great deal of effort into convincing him to make the trip. But didn't he once say that, when he was in East Africa during the war, he'd formed a poor opinion of the Indians serving there? Yes, the memory crystallises, he'd seemed to blame his own sufferings more on the presence of the Imperial soldiers from India and so on, than on the enemy, the army's apparently wholly inadequate preparation or (as he described it) the plague of insects they'd had to deal with. Indeed, now I think about it, that seems to have been the Indians' fault too. Something to do with their cooking.

But that was all silly bluster, really. A story told at dinner after too much to drink. No, he's not really prejudiced against these people, I'm sure. All the same, I'll jolly well be asking him about it, next time I see him.

Magsie

I'm inside now, being rubbed dry. Having my head towelled. That hasn't happened for a while.

"I'm all right. What are you doing that for?"

"Magsie. So much mud. What…"

"I was remembering things."

"Why were you out there?"

"Just getting some air. Some fresh air." I'm towelled a bit more. "It's nice to see you," I say.

"Well." I think she's a bit nonplussed. "Well, it's nice to see you too. Even in this state. But that pot could have broken your leg. Is everything OK?"

"I'm fine. I was thinking about old times. Remembering when Hassan came to the village and stayed with us. He met George's father too." She towels a bit more.

"Who's Hassan, Magsie?"

"Has George never told you about Hassan? Well, I suppose he wouldn't have done. I suppose he doesn't know,

now I think about it. No, I wouldn't really have told him. It was back in, now, when was it…" I'm shivering.

"Maybe tell me a bit later, Magsie. Let's get you dry first." She towels away again, runs a bath and helps me into it. I hear her putting my nightie in the wash. She probably found those dirty things in my bedroom and put them in, too. I hope she didn't. I was going to wash those. But then, why not? Why not let her help? I'm glad that George has a nice wife who helps sometimes.

"He came from Persia." I call from the bath. "You could tell he did. He wasn't like the boys from the village. Or even from town. The other boy was English, though, who came later. He met Hassan here. But he wasn't well."

"Who wasn't well, Magsie?"

"The boy. The other boy."

"The English boy? Who was he?"

"He was from the village, but he'd been away. What was his name?" I think. She waits. "He'd been away and he came back and he saw Hassan here in the village and he couldn't speak. He was crying so much."

"Are you sure he came from Persia, Magsie? Iran?"

"No. India." She gives up at that and so do I, for a bit. I'm tired.

"What are you down here for, then?" I call out.

"To see you, Magsie. I needed to come to London and it's not far to pop out. George sends his love." I think he probably didn't, but I hope he did.

"Will you stay for some tea?"

"Yes. Are you having anything brought round today?"

"No. It's her day off." Is it? I can't remember.

"Well, let me make you something." She cooks me a piece of fish with some potatoes and peas. It's good. Better than that sandwich. I put ketchup all over my peas and eat in my dressing gown with a fresh nightie underneath. Time was I'd never have eaten in my nightclothes, but now… well. The girl does come, one I don't know, but she leaves again when she sees I've got company.

"It's good, this. Thanks, Nastia. I'm glad you came. I was being a bit daft out there." We eat a bit more, quietly.

"You could come and see us, you know, Magsie." She doesn't say 'stay', just 'see'.

"It's too far."

"You could fly."

"Fly? Not these days. I shouldn't wonder if I popped my clogs on the aeroplane. Terrible big loud things they are."

"Magsie! Of course you wouldn't."

"Anyway, that's not for me. I can't be going all the way up there. I'm in this house now and that's it. Everything's delivered for me. The girl comes. I know where everything is. I don't need to be going all the way up there to Scotland, travelling to foreign lands."

"It's hardly foreign, Magsie." She clears the plates. "Why were you talking about that Iranian person before?"

I think. "Hassan? He's not Iranian." She opens her mouth to say something, but I carry on. "1930… something, he came." I tell her about him arriving in town. "He came in on the branch line and said he'd travelled from India." She starts again at that, but I shush her and carry on. "No, he wasn't Indian, but he came from India," I say. "Overland, he said, he'd come all the way as far as France. Then he'd got a little boat across to Portsmouth and got on the train."

Rebecca

It feels so long ago, now, when I was back in London with Uncle Peter, in the Dulwich house with its long staircase window, when one of Ashton's infrequent letters had dropped onto the doormat. I had to read the post out loud to dear Uncle in those days, so it was I who first saw the news that a site supervisor and record keeper was to return from the Indian excavation to England after a bout of malaria. Before I'd even read the passage aloud to him, I'd asked my uncle to offer my services. After much cajoling – involving special cooked breakfasts of smoked salmon, eggs and the best coffee I could find – my uncle finally wrote the letter. Next it was Ashton's turn to be dubious, this time about my lack of experience abroad. He would only agree to it if, first, I went for nothing more than board and lodging, and second, that if I really must come, a man must come with me – he couldn't be worrying about another lone woman on site. It's a dangerous business and a dangerous place and he wouldn't be a caretaker, he said. Despite feeling a little irked by all of this, I thought, *Why not?* It would be more fun with Robert, anyway; in the end I convinced him that we were both wasting away in London. I was seriously lacking excitement, and Robert has never seemed quite happy since the war. I don't know why.

Of course, after this had all been agreed, some time passed before we actually arrived on the sub-continent, during which Ashton had to endure an, 'unconscionable lack of company'. His eyes flickered over me as he said that, just after we arrived, and there was the hint of a smile at the corner of his mouth as he turned away and wiped the sweat from his brow. I still pull my clothes a little more closely around me whenever he's there, trying to put his glances and his sweating face out of my mind. And sometimes I imagine how it would feel if Robert looked at me like that, or at least a more elegant version of it, a look that tells me he wants me as much as I want him.

While the others are discussing the site a week or so after my swim, I kneel down and touch the earth. It's fine, dry and dusted through with fragments of papery roots that crumble between my fingers. It's quite remarkable, really, that the trenches – both the ancient ditches the archaeologists have found and the modern excavation itself – have been cut so true and clean. Equally impressive, I learn that the modern diggers have kept intricately detailed, annotated drawings of the surface plan of each square yard, a new drawing made at each five-inch interval of depth as they remove the earth, or whenever something interesting crops up. Ashton has trained the most promising of the locals to make these records and they're paid much more than their fellows. He picks young boys for the task, of around thirteen or fourteen, considering they have the potential for good draughtsmanship and will be biddable and (I imagine) thinking them more likely to be in thrall to him. His theory seems to run that this level of involvement will trickle through and imbue the locals with a greater understanding of and affinity with the work. This in turn will encourage care and dissuade would-be artefact thieves; although the cynical Colonel thinks that such measures in fact probably won't avert the 'natural instinct' of a digger faced with an ancient trinket worth a year's income. It's for that reason that part of our role is generally to keep our eyes open for any pilfering. That seems very pointless to me, but it does mean I get to stroll about the site and get to know everyone a bit better without Ashton suspecting me of slacking.

As I drop the last of my handful of dusty earth back to the ground, I remember my conversation with Erica and the fact that I haven't yet had a chance to speak to Robert about his comments. I think he suspects something might be up because whenever we're together in company I avoid his eye. I need to do it when we're alone; it's not fair to raise the matter in front of others. But now, at the end of a day on site, I have my chance. The two of us, with Erica (who'd come up from the tents to discuss something with Ashton) are walking down the hill towards the village when, saying she's forgotten a chart, Erica turns round to head back up to the site. Before she leaves, and with a half-smile, she gives my hand a squeeze, but I shake her off awkwardly. As soon as she's out of earshot, I pull Robert closer and we carry on together, falling into step in the easy way that we always have.

We speak about the dig for a while, and about the efforts that are being made, night and day, to find the missing child. About Ashton and what leads a man to his sort of life, searching the modern world for clues about where it came from. We go on like this for some time and now that I have him here alone, I find it hard to raise the subject that I know I must. We drift on to other things... Food, hunting, the time we spent together at

Robert's family estate when he'd shown me how to fly-fish in the river running through his father's land. Standing behind me, holding my arm as I cast, he laughed and showed me how, his arm moving back and forth with the grace of a dancer's, the line drawing perfect curves through the still Scottish air. I can almost feel, again, the cool water and the slip of the salmon as we pulled him out. But dust and sweat and clinging cotton bring me back to myself. Now is the time. Our reminiscing together has been like lying in bed on a weekday morning, deliciously comfortable but always with an impending sense of the unforgiving day coming on, and now I can't put it off any longer; it's time to get up. But be careful, Rebecca, get this right, don't spook him. For a moment I even wonder if I could let it go, forget about what Erica has told me. But no, that's not how I was raised; it's not me. And Robert is too important.

"Robert, the men here…" I hesitate, searching for words. "Do you… like them?" No, that's not right.

Robert stops dead on the track and stares at me. "What does that mean? Do I like them?"

I frown. I'm playing my hand badly. I didn't mean to have an argument, but this is already more aggressive than I'd hoped. "I mean… Do you respect them?" Oh, I'm going to have to come out and say it. "Do you think they're… savages? Erica thought she heard you saying something beastly like that. I really didn't… You don't think that way, do you? I know you had a tough time in Africa, but it wasn't the Indians' fault…" I look at him. "Robert, why are you smiling?" As soon as I said the word 'savages', Robert's tension fell away. "Why are you laughing? This is important. They're people, Robert, they shouldn't be treated like that."

"I couldn't agree with you more," he says, steadying himself. "I thought you meant… something else. Of course I don't think they're savages. Why on earth did Erica think that?"

"I don't know," I say, feeling a little confused. "She thought she heard you saying something about them, when Ashton was droning on about the mound. A few days ago."

Robert frowns. "Really, I haven't the faintest idea," he says, his mood seeming to blacken again. "But I don't see why it would be any of her business, anyway. Who cares if I do think they're savages? Or what I say to anyone in private conversation, for that matter. It's damned foolish women's gossip. If you really knew me... if you knew what..."

I cut across him, now hot myself. "So you're a fan of the men, after all, but our views are irrelevant simply because we're women?" I glare at him, but Robert doesn't answer for a long time.

At last, he raises his hands in an exasperated way, then drops them to his sides, saying, "Look, you really can't go flying off the handle like this. It's unseemly." He pauses again. "And it's not going to get you anywhere."

"Oh, for Christ's sake, Robert!" I cry and march away from him down the hill. Too quickly. I stumble several times but ignore him calling out after me as I go. What on earth does he mean, not going to get me anywhere; was it about him and me? Or about work on the dig? Or even about my life and my chances? Why would he say that? I turn his words over and over, considering them from every angle, all afternoon, all the hot night long and all the dusty morning. But as I worry at them, the words fade, become worn thin, begin to crackle like an overplayed gramophone record until I can barely even recognise the tune any more. *Time to let them go, Rebecca*, I tell myself, *this is about more than some silly throwaway comments; you know him better than that. And anyway, you don't need him to be perfect.*

Magsie

Things are coming back again, after tea. The lady went over there with some high-up soldier or other, she said. Can't remember the name, but anyway, that chap got his comeuppance. Sounded like he deserved it to me – what he did. I can't abide that sort of thing.

"She went with a Colonel. Or to meet a Colonel, maybe," I say to Nastia.

"Who did, Magsie?"

"The girl who came here. The solicitor."

"What solicitor? Do you need a solicitor, Magsie?"

"No, I don't need one. That's all done and dusted, don't you worry." I raise an eyebrow at her to warn her off any probing. I know George wants this house when I'm no longer in it to clutter up the place. I carry on. "The one who came back, after Hassan. She came and said she thought her friend might be in the village. In our house, she thought. And that he'd come after Hassan. She wanted to know what had happened."

"Were these friends of George's, Magsie?"

She hasn't been listening properly and I give her a sharp look, peeved. But then... she did give me a nice bit of fish. And a bath. Can't be too hard on her for not following. I'm probably not telling it properly. "No, not friends of George's. People don't normally make friends with other people who aren't born yet." I think I said it in a meaner way than I'd meant, because she doesn't say anything more and picks up the serving dishes and takes them through to the kitchen. I think about saying sorry, but I don't. "Or is that what they do in Russia?" I ask. A joke might help.

"No, it's not what they do in Russia, Magsie."

There's a long pause while she runs water into the sink. She says, "How are you feeling? Are you OK now?"

"I was OK before. I was only getting some air. It's not nice being in here all the time."

"I'm not sure you were OK. You were soaked. Is one of your quizzes on now? We could watch that for a while if you like."

"You don't need to watch that with me."

We sit for a moment when she's come back into the living room. I grip the handle of my stick and feel the bone of my hand, hard against the wood. I let it go. I don't like that feeling. It's horrid. I pick up the remote for the TV, but I don't turn anything on. Instead I say, "Where's George? Why didn't you bring George?"

"I can't bring him. He's busy at home. He did send his love, I told you."

"You don't need to lie."

"Of course he sent his love. What do you mean?" She takes two steps across the room and takes the remote out of my hand. "Magsie, what do you mean?"

"If he'd send his love why wouldn't he come? He should have come. You came. I don't want to see you."

That's not what I meant.

Rebecca

So keen is the Colonel to prove his idea of the curving mound to us (our being the first new audience members he's had for some time) one morning he sends a digger to either end of the long, main trench with a rope strung between them. It's true that when they each hold their line to the edge of the mound, there's a definite gap between rope and mound at the centre on the hill side, furthest from the sea; the rope being a straight line and the mound a curved one. This measurement, Ashton tells us, is part of what Erica is working on – extrapolating the curving line of the mound to see how closely it correlates to the hill beyond, if at all, or if indeed it might correlate with anything else. It's clear that Ashton is certain what the outcome will be.

"This is a boundary. Boundaries are crucial," he says. "All of human life is about them and these people were no different; whoever controlled the boundary controlled access… to something. I'm not sure what yet… But whoever controls access has power. And for these primitives, where there's power there are gods and where there are gods there's always gold." He pushes a hand through his thick grey hair.

My skin is prickling again and sweat drops from the end of my nose. I rub at it, feeling irritated. "Isn't that a bit... backward?" I ask him. "You've already decided that gold is going to be their most important symbolic substance when you haven't even found what symbols are made from it... if any."

Robert raises an eyebrow at me. I have the sense of him settling in to watch the conversation unfold, as if he were sitting in the dark at the talkies.

"Yes, thank you, Miss Hellings," Ashton says, waving me away without looking at me as he continues to walk along the trench line. He passes a handkerchief over his forehead. "If we dig this section, and completely understand it, we may have some idea of what it protects. That hill is concealing something. I can't dig the whole bloody thing, but if I can find some clue as to where to look..." He tails off, staring at the rising land, yearning.

"But even if it is a boundary, how do you know the important side is the hill?" I ask, not put off by his haughtiness. "Couldn't it as easily be the coast that is the important place? Maybe a sea god or something. I'm pretty sure, actually, that I've heard of more sea gods than... Hill gods."

Ashton thrusts his hands into his pockets, looks up at the sky, looks down, and finally looks at me. "How about Mount Olympus, for a start, young woman? Strange as it might seem, I have learned a little something about this place in the time I've been here. And in the forty years I've been studying the peoples of antiquity." The last words are said with a sneer of contempt. He wipes new runnels of sweat from his face, stuffs the marked handkerchief back into his pocket and glares at me for a response.

"Well, perhaps an outside perspective might be helpful."

"The only thing that would be helpful at this moment is tea, some food and a little less theorising from you if you'd like to stay on my dig." He starts walking back towards the camp during this and the last words are almost shouted as he strides away. He beats the words out on his leg with the riding crop I've seen before. But it strikes me that he's beating his leg with the handle end, with the whip loop again held carefully, even gingerly, just as he was when he sketched out the death faces in the earth. He's a queer old devil and no mistaking.

Robert breaks across my thoughts by applauding quietly, smiling at me. "Now that's swell, Rebecca, old girl. Keep that up and we can go home." He puts his arm around me and gives me a squeeze. Here he is again, again I can secretly imagine he's mine, close to me once more after our silly row. My skin prickles with electricity where his bare forearm touches the back of my neck, where his breath grazes my cheek as he speaks, low, into my ear. Can I simply turn towards him now, put my mouth to his? I play it out in my mind's eye, the way the world falls away all around us as he holds me, everything reducing down to that moment, the two of us. Then it's gone, he's turned and is walking away, calling, "You coming, old girl?" over his shoulder as he goes.

I'm smiling to myself when Erica, who, unknown to me, has been quietly watching this exchange, takes the few steps over to me. "You're in love with him," she says in a quick and rather stern way, and shushing me with a wave of her hand, "don't try to protest. I'm not interested in hearing your denials; they're pointless and they'll only waste time." Goodness, she's even more of a one than I thought. She goes on, "What I *am* interested in is what you're going to do about it." I look down at my hands, open my mouth to speak but shut it again.

"Nothing," Erica says, "that's what I thought," and, taking my hands in her own and smiling at last, she says, "but why? Why aren't you doing anything? Have you ever even tried to tell him how you feel?" What an absurd notion.

"Of course not," I say, and Erica leaps on my words.

"Look, I can't watch you mooning around after him for the whole time you're out here, getting into silly rows and never getting any closer to what you want. It's too, too boring. I know why you're nervous, he's beautiful, even the diggers seem to follow him with their eyes as he walks about in that languid way, but," and this is rather startling, "so are you. You are, please believe me. And you're interesting, and unusual. In a very good way," she says, as I frown at that, "look at you in your trousers and… adventuring all the any out here to India. You're a strong—"

"I'm certainly not that," I say, "and I'm happy" – I'm not – "I don't need to be chasing after Robert."

This is all feeling in equal measure exciting and very, very worrying. What might she do? I can't have her going off and doing something awful like, well, telling him how I feel… or how she supposes I do. My stomach lurches at the very thought. I plead with her not to say anything and to my huge relief, she says after a time, "Look, of course I won't say anything if you don't want me to. What do you take me for?" She puts her hand on my face and smiles at me. "There's nothing to worry about. All we're going to do is create a situation where he realises for himself, not that you love him, but that he loves you." I'm a little staggered by this and grip her wrist with both hands.

"What?" I say. "No, of course he doesn't, how… ridiculous."

"Yes," she says, now taking my hands in hers. "Of course he does. Why do you think he's here with you? And you're so close, look at you both; I'll bet you've been dancing around each other for years." Somehow, I find I can't deny that. "We need only give it the merest nudge," she says, "and I can help with that, leave it with me, you lovely girl." She leans forward and touches her nose to mine.

Magsie

SHE'S QUIET FOR A MOMENT, BUT NOT LONG. SHE'S clever, this girl, and she knows more than what you say most of the time. Sometimes she'll tell you what you mean and you didn't know it yourself. I don't always like it much.

"Magsie, I know you miss him. He will come and visit soon, I promise."

"I don't miss him. He needn't come if he doesn't want to." What am I doing? I fold a little lower in my chair. I'm just getting tired and lashing out. It won't do. I take a slightly ragged breath. "Of course I miss him." I squeeze the tissue in my hand. "Nastia, why didn't he come?"

"I think sometimes…" She pauses. For a long time this time. "I think sometimes he finds it a bit sad. He wants to see you, but coming here, it's too much of the past and," she pauses again, "you're older and… he finds it all too much."

"I find it bloody sad," I say, "that's no reason." I think I understand. A bit. But what about what I feel? We sit for a while.

"Elspeth's upset too," Nastia says. "George doesn't approve of her boyfriend. I don't understand it. He seems a really great guy to me. But I think," she pauses and peers at me oddly, "George thinks he's not good enough because he's not English. Well, he lives in England now. But George..."

She raises her hands in exasperation but peering at me again. I wonder if it's to see whether I'll be prejudiced too.

"Yes, I know all about Aban," I say. "Elspeth writes to me. And I speak to her sometimes on the telephone. Didn't you know? I wanted to talk to George about it on the telephone too, but he had to disappear off somewhere because he was so busy, he said." Nastia looks amazed. "George has always had a few wrong ideas." I say, after I've let her wonder for a bit. "I don't know where they came from, but it wasn't me and it definitely wasn't his dad."

"No, I didn't think so. But... Oh, I can't see a way through it." She runs her fingers through her dark hair and grips it at the back of her head, pulling her eyebrows up. She drops her hands and continues. "Elspeth's so upset. George won't have him in the house. Won't even meet him. Well, not properly. I'm worried Elspeth's going to run away. For God's sake, they might even run off to Iraq or somewhere and who knows what... I might never see her again." We're quiet again for a bit. Nastia wipes at her eye with the heel of her hand.

"She's nearly a grown woman," I say.

"She is one, legally," says Nastia. "She can marry him if she wants to; she's eighteen. I could understand it if there was actually anything wrong with the guy, if he was – you know – a criminal or a, a junkie or something. But he's not. He's lovely. All he's done is lose his home – that's it," she groans. "It makes me so angry. But I shouldn't be telling you all this, Magsie, it's not fair."

I ignore that last bit and say, "So you've met him, then?"

"Yes, a few times. Normally I can talk George round if he's being... Well, you know. But not with this. It's all part of this immigrants thing he has, and refugees, well that's even worse, for some unfathomable reason. As if it's Aban's fault. But I think it would mostly be embarrassment really – he couldn't face his friends in the pub. I mean it's, it's... pathetic, really." She shakes her head. "And my father was Russian, anyway. Ridiculous."

"But you're white." It hangs there for a moment before I carry on, "I expect we'd find all sorts in our family if we went back far enough."

That boy. I never could teach him. I could never get through on some things. Important things. When I was trying to explain why he should be kind to the smaller children, or that girls could be as clever as boys. I don't know what went wrong. And his dad didn't help. Always leaving me to be the strict one while he'd just be around for fun and games. Maybe it was George growing up in a time when he saw everything taken away from his country, or thought that's what was happening, rather than the whole world changing around it. Nearly all for the better, I might add.

It's all very well, all this business, if you're only mean-spirited on your own and with someone who's decided to marry you. Someone who probably already knew the worst. But I can't abide it if it's affecting Elspeth. My beautiful girl. "You need to get him to see sense," I say. I can feel myself getting a bit emotional again. "He can't be hurting our little one. It's not fair."

"She's told him. Very straight. I think it's less hurt and more anger that she's feeling now. That's what worries me, really. It means she might do something drastic. Like when she ran away to London before, you remember. All she wants is her dad's approval, really, but if he won't give it, she's not above doing something – extreme – to punish him. She's always done it." There are real tears in her eyes again and she has to take out a tissue to dab at them. "It's awful at home. And…" She pauses, I think to take control of herself before going on, "George is talking about doing something. With… you know that friend of his, Mick." She looks like there's a bad smell under her nose. Yes, I know Mick, I think, that big sack of a man with his gravel-chip eyes. Always in a monogrammed shirt with great sweat patches, whatever the weather. Nastia continues, "I think he's got into George's head about it, how it's a disgrace or something to let his daughter be with a… well, you know, I'm not going to say the word he uses. I'm scared, Magsie… about what they might do."

Hassan's face appears in my mind. He knew what happened if people wouldn't let you be with someone you loved. He found out the hardest way. George, you're not doing this to my granddaughter. I do love you, but you need a good talking to and no mistake.

Nastia stays for the rest of the day, but she's off before it's dark. Never stays over, that one. Never anyone to wake up with in the house any more. But wake up I do. Another day. But this time, a day with something real to do.

The sun is shining bright around the edges of my leafy curtains. I feel somehow energised as soon as I wake. Scotland. I could go. Could I go? I can help Elspeth. If he sees me – sees that I've come all that way to speak to him. Can I fly? Will I survive it? Will it really matter if I don't? Maybe I'll pack my travelling bag. Just in case. I don't need to do anything with it. Goodness. Where would my travelling bag be?

Slow down, Magsie. Have some breakfast first. You can't be haring about the place on an empty stomach. After a bite of toast and some tea I'm up again to open the thin cupboard at the back of the house. It smells musty and there's a small cascade of, well, all sorts as I pull the door back. Scarves in orange and brown and green patterns, a box of buttons that spills, a lumpy clay pot that George made and painted green when he was a boy. A hat slides down and its brim crumples against the floor. I put it on and glance in the mirror. *Stick to the task at hand, Margaret Brown,* I admonish. Is it in here? I pull away armfuls of silks and knitteds and find the back of the cupboard. Must be somewhere else. Don't think I'll manage it if it's in the attic. Haven't done a ladder for a long time.

Under the bed. Give it a go. Back in my room I look at the old bed frame and the floor and the small gap... this is going to be a little bit tricky. I ease down onto one knee and there's a shooting pain as it takes my weight, but only for a moment. I let the other knee down and, slowly, slowly, roll my body down onto my right shoulder so I'm on my side. I can see under the bed now and there it is: my old leather valise, pushed far under the bed by the wall. I shuffle up to the bed on the floor and reach under it as far as I can with my right arm. Almost. Almost. Stretch a little more. The leather handle feels stiff and brittle under my fingertips. In a few minutes I have the bag in front of me on the bed and somehow I'm upright again. Well, there's a thing. Maybe I can move around a bit better than I thought.

I load all sorts of things – some I daresay I'll need, most I probably won't – into the bag and get on some sturdy, comfortable trousers and some rubber-soled shoes. Airport, that must be next. But how? Am I definitely doing this? What happened to packing just in case? I check my watch. Half-past three. How on earth did that happen? Is it too late in the day to be setting off somewhere? And I need to eat. Surely. No, I'll be fine – they sell food in airports, don't they? I feel myself dithering back and forth and decide I must either go, or stay, right now. *This is one of those moments, Magsie, the big ones.*

I look at the picture of Simon by the bed. He's young and handsome and his eyes are full of love. "Go," he's saying. "Go." Right, I will.

Rebecca

THE FOLLOWING MORNING, I FIND A NOTE PUSHED under my door. My heart races with the thought that it might be from Robert, that Erica might have managed to work some sort of secret magic overnight, but no, it's not from him. Ashton, or one of his small boys, must have delivered it to my hosts late last night or very early this morning. I'd neither heard nor seen anything when I turned in at around midnight and it's only a little after six now. The note is written in a fine and confident hand.

Miss Hellings,
  I must apologise for my haste when last we spoke. I'm afraid I'm so immersed in matters here that I can sometimes forget myself and fly off the handle. It would be very good of you to accept an offer of a little supper on Saturday by way of apology. Do say yes and I shall feel much better. You can send a reply with the boy. I've told him to wait.

Until then, I remain in your debt,

J. Ashton.

Well, Erica will enjoy this. A private supper with the Colonel. I suppose I must go. Or else refuse him and leave the dig and probably India altogether.

But after a minute or two of musing I remember the words, "I've told him to wait." How long has the poor boy been here, for heaven's sake? I quickly dress and leave the house by the front door and, indeed, a very small boy is curled up outside. I gently wake him and send him back to the Colonel with a note to say that I accept his invitation on condition that this boy is given a cooked breakfast and sent home with extra pay. Feeling rather pleased with this and with the boy's smile (though he tries to hide it) as I try to explain to him what my note says, I turn my thoughts to the day's activities and to what on earth Erica might be plotting.

After his fairly intensive introduction to the site, Ashton is keen that before starting work in earnest we should be turned loose into the region for a little while to 'take a taste of it' and, unwittingly, he's given me just the opportunity I want to spend time with Robert – he's not without his good moments. So having taken some tea and eaten a little of the *roti* that has been left out for me with fresh and delicious butter made from buffalo milk, I walk across the village and hammer on Robert's door until he wakes. After the extraordinary conversation with Erica, my mind is whirring with possibilities. Could he really love me? Surely it's impossible. Almost in a daze, I pack up some lunch with a couple of bottles of light wine from Ashton's private store, thinking the water might not be that safe to drink and feeling that a little drop while we're out on our own might, well, ease things along a little.

We look at our options for exploring once Robert has appeared, bleary-eyed. The railway is a limited affair in this part of India, and anyway, we feel like finding our feet quite locally. I've borrowed some maps from the site HQ, which I give to Robert, and I take responsibility for getting us in the mood to start enjoying ourselves. Ashton did suggest that we take a guide, but I'm quite happy to trust to Robert's navigating experience and, in case of anything unexpected happening in terms of wildlife after my fright at the swimming spot, a well-oiled Westley Richards rifle that Robert brought over from England. We set off when the air is still cool, with only a hint of humidity, and walk inland towards the hills. We're unhurried, and quite happy to return the curiosity of the locals – some we find are desperate to give us tea or offer *paan*, or merely to try to talk; others are more reticent.

After a few hours of walking, we're well up into the hills, heading north, and still with a good view of the sea. The air is by now blue-white in the fierce sun and we take some shade by a small surging brook. We put the bottles into the water by the bank, against a firmly-placed log, and set about the food. In the heat we don't need very much and after eating, we pull up one of the bottles. It's so wonderful being alone with him for a day, at last, and I'm afraid I get a little overexcited, becoming drowsy with the wine much more quickly than I'd intended; I was only supposed to be relaxed, not tight. I think I'd better ease off for a while and anyway, it seems sensible to lie out the hottest hours, so we lie and watch the sea and the few small boats scattered across it like peppercorns on a blue tablecloth. While the heat presses down on my body, and I drift on the edge of consciousness a little later, I seem to hear voices quite close to us. A brief murmur, quickly silenced. I think little of it, and after another hour or so – during which I'm sure I fall quite to sleep – Robert sits up.

"Rebecca." He's silent for a long time, looking past me at the dense leaves that seem to teem with life out of view. At last he says, "I'm sorry I've been... I think you've been a better friend to me than I have to you." I open my mouth to interrupt, but he carries on, "I know I'm not always easy. Not always, I don't know, good company. I've never been able to... be..." he looks up into the branches and sky, "easy with other people. But I am with you."

He looks at me and smiles in an embarrassed way. I seem to hear my blood rushing above the hoots and wails of the forest. Is it really happening? Surely not. Surely Erica can't have been right about him... but if she is, could now be the moment?

"Robert..." I begin reaching out towards him, but something seems to change in him.

He takes a step backwards and speaks over me, "How about we try to make the ridge before heading home?"

Almost as soon as it had begun, the moment has gone. I try to get him talking again, to understand what it was that he wanted to say, but he's gone far away again and won't be drawn. So we pack up our bags in silence, lighter now that we've eaten, and make off through the trees and out onto a path of stone and dry, dusty earth. This winds its way up towards a saddle on the ridge-line. The earth peters out the higher we climb and is replaced by loose scree. It's hard going and hot work, and my head swims with heat and wine. Our feet slip over and in amongst the small stones and we have to drag ourselves through each step. I keep looking for a chance to speak to Robert again, but the hill is far higher than it seemed, and the sun presses like lead. Enjoying the challenge, I think, Robert soon has his head down, setting a determined pace, and after a while I give up any thought of recapturing the moment and, like him, I think, lose myself in the rhythm and thick air.

A few hundred yards from the ridge-line I lift my head and drag my hand over my face, the sweat running down my cheeks like hot childhood tears, and think I see a figure ahead. I rub at my stinging eyes and, still walking, stumble against a stone and stagger. I catch myself and, looking again, with no doubt this time, see a tall shape in a sweeping robe and red and white *keffiyeh*, standing quite still and looking down on us.

I don't know why, but I call out to Robert in warning. But he's already stopped and is standing silent as the mountain, staring upwards at the figure. After a few moments, it turns away abruptly and a rifle at its back is silhouetted against the sky. The man steps down away from us over the ridge and disappears.

I try to catch my breath. "Good gracious. What an extraordinary fellow. A shepherd, do you think? Why would he be up here?"

"There's no grass. Goats can't eat this," Robert says. He sinks down to sit amongst the scree and I start as I see that the blood has drained from his cheeks. As he sat, he dislodged a stone and it rattles down the hillside, picking up speed until it cracks into a boulder further down and breaks in two. "He's not a shepherd," he continues. "Have you seen anyone else in that rig? That was an Arab."

I search the curved horizon against the bright sky, but there is no sign of the man and we don't see him again that day. I'm truly weary by the time we reach the top, and don't give the view we find there the admiration it deserves. The hills, we learn from the map, are the Western Ghats, and run for almost eight hundred miles down the side of the subcontinent, pressed against the Arabian Sea. With that ocean at our backs we turn and walk into the Indian interior, looking wild and vivid green from our rocky pass, and staggering in its scale.

Over the weeks that follow, when we have free time, we climb again to this spot, and explore the ridges and summits of other hills near to the camp. I wonder if we will see the Arab again, but it seems he evades us or has moved on. Soon enough, Ashton sees a way to turn our excursions to use.

Magsie

When the taxi comes it's a man called Andy, and he picks up my old bag like it's a feather and drops it in the boot of the silver car. It looks very sad and small in there, and a bit old and dusty. I imagine I look the same when I sit in the back seat.

"Just you is it, Mrs Brown?"

"Yes, just me."

"Gatwick?"

"Yes. Thank you."

Andy tells me about his pottery as we drive along. It's nice for a man to have a hobby, but really, I don't need to hear about it, and I start to drift off as he talks. A long time since I've been in a car. It's like being rocked to sleep. The hum of the road. The feeling of someone else being in control.

I wake with a start. "Simon?"

"Here we are. Nodded off a bit there? I would have done,

too." I look out of the car window. Take a moment. 'Gatwick Airport', says the sign. Right. Yes.

"I did nod off, I'm afraid. You mustn't take it personally," I say, pressing down the feeling that I'd woken up in the old Volvo and the moment of panic when I realise where I am.

"Not at all. Let me get your bag for you."

He looks like he's about to say more, and I don't really want to hear about clay and firing temperatures any longer so I say, "Thank you," a little more loudly than I'd intended, put a note in his hand and turn away. Bugger off now, Andrew.

I wouldn't have had to be doing this if Simon had been around. You can be sure George would have been visiting then. It was different with his dad. But that boy's going to get a visit now that he won't forget. Now, how does this business all work? Good heavens. Long-stay parking. Short-stay parking. Hotels. Arrivals. Departures. I pick up my bag and start to walk towards the building. One step at a time. I reach a bench and lean on it. A man comes over.

"Excuse me, madam. Do you need any help? Where are you going today?"

"I need to buy a ticket."

"Right. Where are you heading?"

"Edinburgh."

"OK. Well you'll need North Terminal departures for Edinburgh." Bloody Andy brought me to the wrong one. The man's still looking at me. "Would you like me to get someone to take you in a buggy?"

I look at him and smile. "Too bloody right I would."

Rebecca

Some time after our encounter with the Arab, Ashton leads the small British contingent up to a bluff above the main site to take stock. "Baker," he says, "you and Hellings are getting a feel for this area. I've been wondering about those hills where you've been walking. If H1" – this is what he has taken to calling the hill apparently surrounded by the long mound – "is so important, these could be too. We should investigate, see if it's unique or part of a bigger local pattern. I want you two to survey the whole area. Start with H1…" He pauses, and with a slight smile says, "No. Let's give her a proper name. We'll call this one Saraswathi. How's that?"

I frown, then Ashton surprises me: "For all your wanderings, you haven't picked up much about these native fellows have you, Hellings? Saraswathi's the goddess of wisdom and, as it happens, wife of the big chap: Brahma. I'm pretty sure you've heard of him. Saraswathi is knowledge and truth to these people and she's exactly what we need to find up there."

Ashton has even caught Robert's ear with this, but I'm a little dubious and venture, "Are you sure that's… respectful? Would the men like it, the hill being named after their goddess like that?"

Ashton looks at me for a moment, with a blank, uncomprehending face, and continues, "So, you chaps, er… you, er… you two take say, twenty men, systematically search along the line of the mound to start with, working your way inland. When you reach the valley on the far side, split your line. Baker, you move west, Hellings east. Work your way along the coast. We'll see how far we get. And both of you take two runners. Any artefacts you find, map their location and get them down to me at double time. If it seems important, I'll send up more men. Well, see to it."

Business done, he mops his brow and steps smartly off to his quarters. Ashton typically sleeps early, having exhausted himself each day, though he hides it well behind his habitual military bearing. Once he's gone, Robert arches an eyebrow at me.

"Funny old bugger, he is. Didn't expect a sentimentalist. 'Mount Ashton', I'd have expected, or 'Mount Windbag'. 'Mount Booze-Addled-Old-Idiot'. On which note, shall we have a drink?"

The dig and our survey progress comfortably the next day. We stick well into our work and are absorbed with managing the teams. When Ashton first raised the walking survey, I'd thought here might be another chance of snatching time alone with Robert, but in fact it seems clear that we are always to be amongst the men. I urgently want to speak to Erica again, to tell her about that moment Robert and I had shared up on the mountain and to see what she thinks of it, whether there'd been something real there or if I'm imagining things. And if it is something real, what we might be able to do about it. It's such turmoil believing one moment that he might feel for me – love me, even – and the next that I'm the stupidest, silliest person even for thinking it. Oh, it's awful, why did you have to say those things, Erica; why couldn't you just leave me with my happy imaginings? It's so much harder when there's hope, and now I feel sick with it.

I come firmly back to earth when Ashton reminds me of our supper engagement. I didn't mention it to Robert at the time, but I'm forced to do so when Ashton's, "Remember, Miss Hellings, seven-thirty tomorrow," is hallooed over the trenches at me in front of everyone.

"I couldn't have said no, Robert," I protest, in a whisper. "It would have been tantamount to resignation."

"Well, I hope you enjoy it," he grimaces.

Shortly before the appointed time, the same small boy returns to collect me from my lodgings. There's no trace of his smile this time and he walks me in silence the short distance to Ashton's billet. The Colonel also shares with a family, but they have retired to one very small room at the back of the house next to the kitchen and have left the remainder of what is one of the larger properties in the area to their overbearing tenant; I hope they are suitably recompensed for what can't be a comfortable arrangement. The room we're in holds no trace of the Indian family, but the Colonel's influence is everywhere; army portraits, boxes of finds, a sabre (who knows what he thinks he might need that for), two *sola topi* helmets (one fairly soiled, the other much cleaner), and a general meticulous tidiness and order.

"Miss Hellings. Come," he says, on the boy's knocking and opening the door. "How pleasant. I see you're still in your trousers. Well. Good." Ashton doesn't rise for a few moments after I arrive but, at last, pushes himself up from his chair and strides to a side table near to where I stand. "May I prepare you a drink?" Ashton's man makes us each a gin and tonic – with no ice – and is curtly dismissed.

"Now, Miss Hellings" – I don't feel it necessary to permit him to call me Rebecca – "I wondered if I might tell you a little more about why we're here." He does so, at length. I can't say I'd expected a lecture when I agreed to come here, but now it seems that this is the price I'll have to pay for my supper. I realise my thoughts have wandered a little when I notice he's saying, "Does that sound credible to you?"

I look at him. "I'm sorry?"

"The New Culture narrative. Do you believe it?"

I have scant idea what he's been talking about, but this does ring a bell from what Erica was saying when we first arrived here. All the same, I'm going to have to try to dodge the question and I venture, "Yes. But have you asked anyone who... any other archaeologists?"

This turns out to be a lucky move, as he wags a finger and says, "Ah yes. Now there's the question. That's who one has to convince, of course. The discerning minds. Although, speaking frankly, there are only a few discerning minds within modern archaeology." Obviously, he is chief amongst them. "But the wife's the one whose views I'm really worried about," he says, without a trace of irony, "She's twice the mind of most of the dullards out there digging today. I often think she has a sight more of a brain on her than me." I open my mouth to speak but shut it again. The old fellow is married, devoted even. Now here is something juicy to tell Robert and Erica.

"I run all my manuscripts past her first," he goes on. "She's my editor. Knows nothing of archaeology really – although I suppose she's picked up bits and pieces by now – but she can shine a light through a weak argument like no-one else. I remember she once took apart a paper I'd written on the

Bronze Age fens like it was tissue. In the end I scrapped the whole thing; couldn't publish a word of it." He sloshes his gin at this point and hammers on the table for his glass to be refilled.

"But don't you miss her," I ask, "being here in India for so long?"

"I do miss her, Hellings, but that's the life of a soldier. Even a retired one. One carries one's loved ones around the place of course, in one's memory and," he produces a leather photograph frame, "one has pictures." He holds it out to me. It's a picture of a much younger woman than Ashton and I take it to be an old photograph. Indeed, it looks like a silver daguerreotype, perhaps from the time they were married. Even so, the woman must still be handsome now, if she has kept her looks. Dark curly hair and a fine brow, her eyes turned slightly away from the camera.

"She's beautiful," I say.

"Oh, do you think so?" He looks at the picture for a moment, then sets it back down on a leather travelling chest next to the paraffin lamp that is providing all the light we have. As he pushes back his thick grey hair with his usual mannerism, he says, "I should like to know a little more about you now, Miss Hellings. You've never married?"

Slightly startled by the question, I answer that I haven't, but hope to one day.

"Well, I shouldn't think it will be to the young lieutenant," he booms.

I feel my face burning. "I don't think I like…" I begin, but splutter into bewildered silence. He raises an eyebrow at me, but at that point Ashton's man returns to say our food is ready and we go through to another room lit by two lamps turned up high. As we sit down, I decide to let the point go. I can't think of anything Ashton might have to say about Robert that would interest me and, anyway, I'm not delighted at the prospect of a fuller exploration of the topic of my spinsterhood. Ashton seems happy to move on too and introduces our menu for the evening with what seems like real delight. We settle down to eat and drink, with Ashton's man pouring wine.

"Bit of a challenge, the local scoff, but I've got my chap trained up to cook the proper way too, for when I fancy it," says the Colonel.

The meal is duck with a decent effort at roast potatoes, followed by a fruit pie. On safe topics, I find to my surprise that Ashton can be good company, and a couple of glasses of passably cold white wine into the proceedings, on top of a healthy amount of gin, I almost start to enjoy myself. I recall the pretty wife and manage gently to steer the conversation back in her direction.

"Oh, Daisy. Yes, well, she was always rather bright. Did well at school and thought about university, even, but her father wouldn't have it. Then we married and…" Ashton looks into his glass for a long moment. "And she was going to… go to work; she wanted to write, but that was never really on the cards."

He pushes his glass away and looks directly at me. "I suppose there's no harm in telling you. We wanted to have a child. But we couldn't. Don't know why; doctors couldn't say. We thought once that she might be… but. Well, that's that." He drains his glass and motions to the man to open another bottle. "Daisy's happy now, and we have the dogs. A number of dogs, in fact." He laughs at the mention of them. "Lovely chaps. Do you keep dogs, Miss Hellings?"

"No," I say. "I never have, I'm afraid. I've always been a little… disconcerted by dogs. They don't seem natural, somehow, being made by breeders into all different shapes and sizes like that."

"Stuff and nonsense," says the Colonel, waving a hand at me. "They're still natural beasts inside. Same instincts, but with some of the baser ones kept at bay. And they're great fun, d'you see. A lovely greeting you get in the morning and when you come home. Yes, I shall be back for a visit to see the old girl and the beasts before too long. You were quite right, I do miss her. Something rotten." He smiles. "But it's getting late, Miss Hellings. We shall be sleepy in the morning. Let me see you out."

Before he closes the door, he says, "Miss Hellings, I wonder if you wouldn't mind keeping our conversation this evening private. I rather keep Daisy to myself while I'm over here. Doesn't do to let the men know too much about one's personal life, you know." The door shuts behind me and the dark night air is surprisingly cold, so I pull my jacket around me, glad that I didn't bother wearing a dress for dinner.

Before I go to bed, I write a short note that I mean to slip to Erica the next chance I have: "Need to talk. Swimming bay at five o'clock. Come alone. R."

Magsie

We buzz through the airport buildings with my little buggy peeping at everyone to get out of the way.

"Thank you!" I call at some of the friendlier-looking ones as we go. Most people don't look altogether pleased at having to move out of the way as they struggle along with their bags, but I get a few smiles. Mostly from ladies, but one from a nice-looking man with a sleeping baby strapped to his chest. "I need to buy a ticket," I say to the driver, "do you know where I need to go?" He drops me off at an almost queue-free desk and I ask the lady for the next flight to Edinburgh. She asks when I'd like to travel. "Now," I say, "as soon as I can. I'm all packed." I point to my bag next to me on the floor.

"Right, let me take a look for you." She taps away a little. "The next departure for Edinburgh is a British Airways flight at seven twenty-five tomorrow morning. Shall I book you onto that one? There are plenty of seats available." Oh. That's a blow.

"It's only six o'clock. Is there nothing today?"

"I'm sorry, madam. Nothing direct."

I pay with a cheque, which makes the lady raise her eyebrows a bit, but she takes it slowly in the end and prints out my ticket. I don't know what's wrong with a cheque. Maybe she expected me to beam the money at her with a laser or whatever people do with these phones nowadays.

I walk away from the desk. Well. Much as I'd like to burst in on George and surprise him when I get to Edinburgh, I do have a bit of sense; I'd better phone ahead.

"George? It's your mother." I've got to just tell him it's happening. Brook no opposition.

"Mum? Hi. What's... er... is Nastia with you?"

"No, she's gone now. I'm not at home. I'm coming to see you." There's silence on the line. "Hello? George? Are you still there?"

"Yes, yes, I'm here. What do you mean, coming to see me?"

"I'm at airport, I've bought a ticket, there's no two ways about it now, I'll have to stay a couple of days. That's all, so I'll see you in the morning."

"What, hang on, Mum, don't hang up. You can't... what's all this about? I mean..."

"What's it about?" That hurts a bit. "I'm coming to see my son and my granddaughter."

He breathes out loudly down the line, and says, "Look I'm not trying to... you can't just turn up."

"Why not? It's Saturday tomorrow. You're not doing anything, are you?"

"No, but..."

"Well then." There's another long pause.

"I'll be... look, I'm going out tomorrow." I start talking again, but he carries on, speaking over me, "Look, look, don't get excited, I'll be at home in the morning, I'm only out in the afternoon. Make sure you're there before eleven-thirty, OK, or I won't be there, I'll be… on a coach away to Leeds to the cricket. I'm not going to wait for you."

"Who with?"

"What?"

"Who are you going to the cricket with?"

There's a pause, then, "Mick. What does it matter?"

"Fine. Bye."

Mick. Going to the cricket, my foot. George has never been to a cricket match in his life. He's not even interested in sport, never has been. I have a sick feeling at the thought of what they might be planning to do. And I can't help feeling sad for me, too. Why is he like that with me? I'm trying; I've always tried to be a good mum to him. I look around me at the huge empty spaces of the airport.

Now you're in a pickle, Magsie. Nowhere to go all night and no way to get to Edinburgh until morning. But I did see that sign saying, 'Hotels'. I should find somewhere to stay. And somewhere to eat. My stomach's grumbling. It will all seem a bit better if you have a bit of food, I tell myself. You know where I haven't been in a long time? A pub. There must be one somewhere around here. Aren't there always news stories about people being drunk in airports? Or is it on planes? Anyway, let's see what we can see. Simon would have sniffed out the beer by now. "Let's go and have a drink, old boy," I murmur to him.

I look around for my friend with the buggy, but he's nowhere to be seen, and I can't hear him peeping either, so I start walking. I feel so much stronger than at home. My legs are less stiff. Still a bit of a twinge in the knees, but I feel I could walk a mile. I make my way slowly through a big hall full of desks with bright signs above them with the names of airlines. Nice British Airways. Horrid shiny, budget ones. The room moves gently by and I can hear something a bit boisterous-sounding round the corner at the end past the row of doors at the entrance. 'The Flying Pig'. Well, it'll have to do. I have a rest on a bench halfway there.

"A bottle of red, please. House will be fine. One glass." The bartender looks at me for a moment and reaches down a bottle of merlot and a glass. I pay and take it off to a varnished wooden booth with a view through the window of, well, not very much. *I shall get gently sozzled*, I think, and I have a gulp. It's not bad. By about a third of the way through the bottle I'm starting to feel that warm fuzziness inside that I haven't felt for years. I don't keep any booze in the house. But that does feel good, now. As I'm topping up, a waiter comes over.

"Anything to eat this evening?" I hadn't noticed the menus on the only slightly sticky table.

"Yes," I say. "What's good?" He looks at me blankly. I think he's trying to figure out what old ladies eat.

"Um. A burger?"

"I'll have a burger, then. And some chips."

"Burger with fries." He keys it into something that looks like a calculator. "Any sides? Coleslaw?"

"No, thank you." I suspect the burger, when it comes, is not the best example going, but to me it tastes wonderful. The tables around me have now filled up completely. Closest to me is a family with suitcases piled up behind them. Tanking up the kids before the long journey. Slightly further away on my other side are three young men. I think they're talking about politics.

A bit more than halfway down my bottle and around an hour and a half later, I'm feeling quite odd. Maybe I'll leave the rest. George has left me feeling foolish again, he always does that, and the food and drink didn't help as much as I thought it would. I wonder what Elspeth's doing. The barman directs me to a pay phone; I tinkle in a few coins and dial her number.

"Elspeth?"

"Granny! Hi." She makes a loud kissing sound into my ear. "How are you?" I still find it strange that she has that lovely Scottish accent.

"Hello, love, it's noisy there, are you out and about?"

"Just in town, I can't speak long. Is everything OK?"

"Yes, I'm OK. I spoke to your dad, he's…"

"Is he being a scunner again?" Her voice is flat.

"Elspeth," I start, thinking that whatever a scunner is, it can't be good, "you shouldn't…" but I lose the will and say, "yes, he is, really. But I'm on my way up to see you and I'm going to give him a talking to."

I don't want to get into why I'm going up, don't want to spoil her mood on her night out, so I quickly move on and tell her I'm in the pub with my friend Monsieur Merlot. She laughs.

"Granny, you're pissed. Is that why you're coming up?"

"No, no, I wanted an adventure, silly girl. Though if I am a bit tipsy that's my business." I can see her smiling down the phone, probably in her raggedy old jeans, with that beautiful dark hair she got from her mum.

"But I shouldn't keep you, Ellie, love, you'll want to get back to your friends?"

"No, let them wait," she says, "we've all had a bit of a falling out anyway."

"Oh? Nothing bad, I hope?"

"No, nothing bad." She goes quiet for a moment, maybe wondering whether to get into it with me or move on. She says, "Maybe you can help. Tim – he's this greasy guy from college." I hear her say, "What? You are greasy," presumably to Tim, then she comes back to me, "Tim thinks that there's nothing to be learned from history and that politicians should just think about the problems of their own day, which can't possibly have existed in the same form at any time in the past."

"Right," I say. There's a warm glow in my chest as I listen to her speaking.

"But I've been saying that it's incredibly dangerous not to understand the historical context of modern political decisions."

"Yes," I say. "Well, that sounds right." Still glowing, I'm also feeling a bit bamboozled by this and quickly try to gather myself, saying, "I'd think that everything people are worried about today has really happened before, in one way or another." Getting going now and feeling unusually eloquent with the wine coursing round my system, "People get better at things with practice, don't they; they need to experience things, learn and do them again, better. Think about an athlete. Do you think anyone ever wins a gold medal their first time on the track? No. They practise and learn. It's the same thing, really. Why have I gone all echoey?"

"Sorry, Granny, I've put you on speaker. They need to hear this."

She shouts something I don't catch, and someone else's voice, a young man's, comes on: "Now come on, er..." It pauses.

"Magsie," I say.

"Magsie. Hi. Nice to meet you. But an athlete training is not the same thing as global politics at all." The last two words he says very slowly and very deliberately.

"OK. So tell me what's unique about this age. What's so different that it's never happened before?"

I hear a 'clonk' sound at the other end of the line, which I think is him putting something on a table.

"This."

"I can't see that, dear."

"Ah. No. Sorry. It's an iPad." I think I've seen one of those advertised on the television. He goes on, "Nothing like this has ever existed before. Nothing even remotely like it until the late twentieth century." I have the sense that he's wagging it at me.

"So what does it do?" I say in my most unimpressed voice.

There's a moment of bewildered silence from Tim, and Elspeth whoops and says, "You tell him, Granny!"

I wink at her down the line before Tim finds his voice again, "Everything. Really. Everything. It's a camera; I can email. But I guess the main thing is that it's on the internet. I can access the whole world from anywhere. More information than I could possibly read or even imagine in a lifetime. All from here. Right now." I hear the clonk again and I think he's whacked the pad thing down, emphatically.

"So it's for communicating. It's for people to communicate with," I say.

"Yes. But in a way that no-one's ever done before."

I think Elspeth feels I might need a little help now, as she says, "I'm tagging in. Tim, how people choose to communicate doesn't affect what life means. What's important is the substance of the communication. It's a tool. Like you." I love hearing her holding her own like this, it's wonderful, and almost makes me forget for a while the horrid mess she's in.

Rebecca

Feeling invigorated and lucid the following day, despite a slight thickness in the head, the armed man from the mountain floats up again in my mind and I broach the subject with Robert: "Have you seen our Arabian friend again?"

"No." Robert is suffering more than I am from the indulgence of the previous evening; he went on drinking with some of the diggers whom he'd befriended.

"Erica told me that there had been a man spotted in the forest around here, and that he might be dangerous. They think he might have done something… with that little girl who's missing. Do you think it could be him? You were very sure he was an Arab."

"I can spot one pretty well," he says. "But with a young girl, you say? No that's not our man."

"How do you know?" I ask, faintly shocked at his certainty, but he stands abruptly and strides away. I watch him go, wondering, but quickly remember my note and call over one of the boys, commanding him to take it to Miss Conston at once.

We continue our hot, dusty, walking survey later that morning and Robert, perhaps starting to feel more human and a little sorry for storming off, tells me that he knew a Persian family during the war who by some quirk of fate had settled in East Africa. Picking up a stick and occasionally thrashing at the undergrowth with it as he speaks, Robert goes on, "They weren't welcome, I never quite knew why. Not many Arabs in Persia, maybe that's all it was. They'd only ended up there in the first place because of the father's work. He was something or other in the silver trade. They'd already had one great upheaval from their real home country by the Red Sea, and off to Persia, looking for trade. Africa was an easy enough next step for him; travel was in his blood. But the rest of them weren't too sure, the children were outsiders already when they were growing up, dressed differently, looked different, and old man Dariush says, 'We're off again,' and they all have to jump." I don't dare interrupt Robert as he goes on; this is the most he's opened up in weeks and it's wonderful simply to listen to his quiet voice telling stories from his past. "Dariush used to do some of his smithing himself, on occasion. Big man, he was, with a big white beard, and he used to do the queerest thing when he talked to you, rolling his eyes up into his head so you weren't sure he wasn't about to pass out on the spot." Robert drops his stick and laughs and imitates the habit, talking with his chin jutting forward and only the whites of his eyes showing then flicking them fully open at times for dramatic effect. "He wouldn't pay me, Mr Robert. Beautiful silver work for him and no money forthcoming! So I say to him, you give me what you owe or I'll put you into my bloody fire! You in there and my bellows… you know where I'll put my bloody bellows, damn you!"

My head hurts as I laugh, and I rub my forehead with my fingertips. "It sounds like he was a good friend."

"Yes. He was for a while. But it was his son who... who I spent time with really. We did a lot together." After that, Robert becomes quiet again, even sombre. I can't pin down what caused the change, but he clearly doesn't want to be drawn any further, and I think better of pressing him; he always was moody. Anyway, we're soon interrupted by a great whooping commotion from further down the line. We have spread our team of surveyors across a wide section of the hill above the mound line, and it seems that one of the men to the extreme right has found something. That end of the line has reached a point at which the hillside dips into a steep gully. I shout to the men to keep their positions, so as not to miss any section when we start the walk again; I'm fairly certain that Ashton's strategy isn't going to come up with the treasures he's seeking, but am determined to survey as well as I can nevertheless. Robert and I run the few hundred yards to the source of the excitement, with (to a man) all the surveyors following behind – evidently my authority is somewhat lacking.

This part of the hill is relatively lush, and the gully seems to have been carved by a stream that, while now slow, was evidently more vigorous in the past. Partly concealed in the bank is a burrow a few inches across, and amongst the spoil cast about lies a fragment of something that is unmistakably made from bronze, oxidised to a blue green. A face stares out from the smooth surface, of far higher quality than those Ashton has found. Even from across the gully we can see eyes, slender nose, narrow mouth; not a skull face exactly, but with something of death about it, in the hollow cheeks beneath high bones, and eyes that seem almost like sockets. It's in quite low relief, on a broken section of what must have been an urn of some sort. Robert leaps across and, picking up the face without much apparent thought to the usual careful recording process of where artefacts are found, plunges it into the slowly moving water. Now washed clean of soil and shining, when he holds it up I feel the hairs rising on the back of my neck, so clear is the face and so lifelike. Is this the first time it has seen the light since before Christ? The day is advancing, and, directing two men to mark the spot, I carefully place the green face in my satchel. Ashton asked us to send a runner if we should find anything, so he would know at once, but, having covered good ground (and, if I'm honest, not wanting to miss out on our share of the backslapping), we decide to head back to the excavation and deliver the news ourselves.

When we find the Colonel, we're not disappointed by his reaction. Taking the face in both hands, he carries it into the map tent and sets it on his usual table. He sinks slowly into his chair, never taking his eyes from the smooth green ones looking back at him. After a few minutes he looks up with a gentle smile and says simply, "Well done."

Almost immediately, once Ashton has surrendered his lover's grasp of the prize, drawings begin of the face from every angle, and each detail of its discovery is noted down. Ashton, having sated himself, strides out of the tent to thoroughly interrogate the man who made the discovery, who gives his name as Singh. Realising at this point that time is getting on rather, I steal a glance at my wristwatch. *Heavens, I think, if Erica received my note, she'll be on the way down there already.* So I slip away from the excited crowd and make off through the forest. I am alone again, and more nervous this time of what might be lurking amongst the dark trees and undergrowth, but I know Erica will be waiting for me and I can't risk anyone else being there, not even one of the locals. When I emerge back into the light of the beach, I squint around me, looking for my friend. It seems for a moment that she has failed to arrive but, with a little burst of relief, I see her stand up from where she's been sitting amongst some smooth rocks and the outermost trees of the forest.

"Well," she says, "here's a bit of cloak and dagger. Is everything well?"

I assure her that it is but find it hard to confess my reason for summoning her like this. The discussion that seemed so essential when I was well-fortified by Ashton's gin and wine now feels the most absurd of ideas. "Erica, I… um…" I press my hands together before my face. "I wanted to… Oh, don't look so amused, it's difficult."

"You want me to help you with Robert," she says. "Don't worry. Like I said, anyone can see you're keen on him, and he on you, but it's not going to happen unless we step up the action."

"Oh, no, no. I didn't mean I wanted to… I only wanted to talk, to tell you what happened."

"Oh," she says, looking excited, "do tell," but when I explain the moment we'd had, when Robert had opened up, there on the mountainside, she seems disappointed. "I thought you were going to tell me that you'd made some progress, actually done something," she says, "but all you've done is moon around hopelessly a bit more." I must admit I'm a little hurt by this; it was a breakthrough, wasn't it? It had certainly felt like one. Realising that she's upset me, I think, Erica squeezes my arm. "Look, I'm sorry, I don't mean to be hard on you, but it's time for action. I'm taking it out of your hands."

"But… how?" I say, feeling a knot growing in my stomach again.

"Don't you worry about that," she says. "I've already cooked something up." *Could she*, I wonder, *could she really pull it off?* With some cajoling, which I think she enjoys, I convince her to tell me every detail of her plan and for a little while, it really does seem possible that it could work. Despite the hot embarrassment I feel even at the thought of attempting it, and terror at the chance that it might frighten him off forever, I start to hope, really hope and, more importantly, believe that it could happen. But all too soon that bright moment is blighted.

I'm still buzzing with excitement about Erica's plan the following morning, when Singh accompanies us to the hillside gully and is again put to describing exactly how he made his find, his story growing with the telling. The entire excavation group, apart from a skeleton staff at the tents, has decamped up the hill and immediately sets about a new and substantial trench, in the process removing the creature whose burrowing had unearthed the ancient face in the first place. That animal turns out, much to my surprise, to be a vivid frog with a protruding snout. It is taken away hurriedly by the diggers, to what fate I cannot guess.

After watching the work for a while, I notice that the Colonel has taken Singh some distance away from the excavation and is speaking to him in a low but savage voice.

"I know you found more of that. Why isn't there any more? That was a fragment; the rest of the vessel must be somewhere. What did you do with it? You'll give it to me. Now." Singh clearly has only a small idea of what the Colonel means and his eyes flash wide as Ashton pulls his riding crop from his belt. "You will tell me, you bloody impudent black-blooded bastard!"

Ashton slashes at the man's face, who staggers back against a tree, a red welt blossoming on his cheek. The Colonel feels at the end of the crop with his fingers, fiddling with something, before shouting, "Now we'll have you." Where Ashton's next blow falls it draws a line in the man's side, where he's turned away, and after a moment, from the line runs a curtain of blood. Ashton strikes him again, slicing across the small of Singh's back. The man screams as his blood spots the dusty earth. But Ashton goes after him as he backs away, falling. The crop strikes again and again as we stand, frozen and terrified, as Singh's very skin seems to disappear beneath the blows.

"Please, Huzoor," someone shouts, but Ashton ignores him, now slashing at Singh's face as he turns in desperate appeal. One of the man's eyes disappears in a ghastly splash of red and white. Something flies from the end of the crop as Ashton pulls it back to strike again. It lands at my feet and seems to break my desperate trance. I come to my senses in a rush, the sound of the world flooding back in, and run towards the Colonel, with Robert joining me as I go, and, gripping the back of his shirt, pull him bodily away from the man on the floor.

Magsie

I should be getting back to my table; I'm getting a little dizzy as I make my way through the glass of wine I brought with me to the phone. And there's now a load of chatter on the line; I can't hear Elspeth properly. I try to shout that I'm going now, that I'll speak to her later and then the line is clear again, she's there.

"Sorry, Granny, that all got a bit out of hand. Tim's daft about that iPad."

"Oh, that's OK." I can't say it's not a relief to have her back to myself again. "So that thing's..." I grope for a word, "...good, is it? Where'd he get it?"

"Anywhere. Everyone stocks iPads these days. Apple stuff is expensive though. You'll be getting cheaper tablets on the market soon. They'll just be a bit more shit. Or Tim said he had a mate who got his from lost property in a hospital. Just went and said, I've lost a silver iPad – chanced it – and they handed one over. No questions asked."

"Goodness," I say, "that seems a bit off." But then again, why not, if someone was silly enough to lose it?

"Yup," goes on Elspeth. "Said it had been handed in earlier that day."

"And he kept it?" I ask, my mind whirring. It seems wrong in a way, but at the same time, it doesn't at all. Maybe it's the wine thinking. I wonder about what Simon would say, but he seems hazy, I can't quite picture his face, can't keep my mind on track, where's the aeroplane, no that's not tonight, it's tomorrow, need to get to bed, get to the hotel. Elspeth's saying something, talking to me: "Granny, granny, are you still there? Are you all right?"

"I'm OK," I say. "Sorry, dear, I've had a bit," I do a bit of a burp, "my mind was… Don't worry, it's all OK, it still works, the brain."

"Granny," she says, "really, why are you coming up now? Is something the matter?" She sounds so serious.

"Oh, I don't want to go into all that now, Ellie, not when you're having your night out; you should get back to your friends."

"Look, Granny, you have to tell me now. I'm not going to enjoy anything; I'll just be worrying. What is it? Are you ill?"

"No, no, I'm fine," I say, rubbing at the worn seat with my free hand and taking another long drink of wine. "It's… well, I'm going to talk to him about you and Aban."

"Oh," she's quiet for a long time before she says in a low voice, "you don't need to do that, Granny, that's for me to sort out."

"I'm not interfering, Ellie, I only want to help you, he's messing everything up, and—"

She cuts me off. "I know what he's doing, but you can't go flying all up the country and upsetting everyone even more."

"I'm not." How does she not understand this? "I'm not upsetting anyone. He is. He's always thought he was better.

And there's..." even as I start to explain it sounds so frail, so pointless, "a story I want to tell him, from when I was little."

I think my voice must have gone very small and sad because Elspeth sounds full of concern again when she says, "What story, Granny?"

I try to tell her but there's a lump in my throat and I can't get it out. I try again. "It's... about someone I used to know, who was so beautiful and he should have got his love, he did have it but he lost it... and it was all for no reason... because people wouldn't accept it. Thought it wasn't right, wasn't natural." I'm crying properly now. "And it can't happen to you, not you, my lovely girl, I won't let it." I sob down the line, not able to speak anymore and I can hear my little girl crying too. I didn't want to upset her. Silly old fool. But I have to help, have to do what I can. "Look, Ellie," I control myself, steady my voice, "I know your dad doesn't like him because he's from Iraq."

"He's lost everything," she says. "He was lucky to get out alive."

She sounds really angry now, but I carry on, "But your dad's got a good heart somewhere in there. I just need to give him a talking to. Set him straight."

"He's a bloody racist, Granny," she almost shouts. "It's my life, I can choose who I want."

"Of course you can," I say, but she says something that troubles me.

"But he won't let me." There's something in her voice, something like defeat, that makes me more worried than I'd been before. I'd always thought that if it came to it, she'd choose the boy, make her own way, but it sounds like the hold George has over her might be stronger than I'd realised.

"Look, Ellie," I say, "your mum's worried that you'll run off with him if it comes to it. If it does... if it does come to it, if you want my advice, that's exactly what you should do." I hear an intake of breath at the other end, but carry on, "You don't get many chances and your dad being a bully is too silly a reason to throw Aban away over. It's your own life, and your own mind you've got to make up." She starts saying something, but I talk more loudly. "And if it does go wrong between you, it'll have had nothing to do with him being from Iraq." Finished, I let her speak.

"Granny... I can't... he's my dad. Look, I have to go, the others are waiting for me. Bye, Granny." She hangs up.

Bugger. Silly girl, she's scared of leaving, and still scared of her dad, I could hear it in her voice. Little girls and their dads. I shake my head. But she shouldn't give in to that sort of thing. I go back to my table and pour out the rest of the bottle. I feel a bit better for having spoken to her, but it's even clearer now that she can't handle this herself. I drain my glass and whack it down on the table a little harder than I'd meant to. It hits the edge and tumbles onto the floor, exploding in shards and wine dregs.

I see Hassan again, in my mind's eye, digging. Turning up the earth. Reaching down into it with those hard hands of his. He'd worked all his life, you could tell. Sometimes you'd see him turn up a clod of earth and rub it away to nothing between his fingers. Watching it fall and disappear back into the field. He studied it so closely as he did it. It was like he was reading the soil. Feeling connected to something.

I try to stand. While I was speaking to Elspeth and her friends, I somehow forgot who I am, and how old. I was almost one of those young people at the pub but as I try to lift myself up, my head swims and here they are again, those knees that don't work, the pain in my hand as I try to push up from the chewing-gummed airport chair. How did I get so old?

"It's OK," I say to myself. "I'll make it. Take it slow, that's all. Get to bed." With a lurch I realise I haven't even got a hotel room yet. I must look really bewildered because the barman comes out to ask if I'm all right. He's just come off his shift and offers to help me find somewhere to stay. He finds a man with another buggy and comes with me to find a hotel. I book a room, lean heavily on the reception desk and breathe for a bit. Again, I remember the young people, how positive they all were, how excited, how in the world, with all their technology and their views. How it felt to be one of them again, even for a moment. I want to feel that feeling again. I grip my stick with my old hand that looks so bony and make my way over to the lifts. I press the call button, but when the lift pings and the doors slide open, I turn back to the desk. Let's be young one last time.

"You haven't had a silver iPad handed in by any chance?"

Rebecca

When I pull Ashton away, allowing Singh to make his escape helped by his fellows, the Colonel stumbles to the floor, but scrambles immediately up again and turns on us, swinging his crop as if it were the sabre from his rooms.

"Hellings." He checks himself when he sees who it is, but his face is red and blotched with rage. "What the devil are you doing? Get back to the camp," he shouts. "This is no concern of yours. And you, Lieutenant, you should damn well know better."

"It jolly well is a concern of mine," I say. "If you touch him again, I'll report it. I'll write to *The Times*."

Ashton sags a little and his face softens and pales, the blotches fading. Some of the men begin to drift away but many remain to watch. "Miss Hellings. The editor and readers of *The Times* would not be at all interested in the fate of this man." He turns and gestures at Singh, who is being supported some yards away by two other men. "And really, there's very little profit in you being interested in him either." I start to speak, but he cuts me off. "His life is brutal and this is the language he understands. Like a dog, you show him love, but you must also show him the whip. If a man needs a tickle, I'll damn well tickle him if I please. And we'll have no more of it now." He turns to the assembled diggers and shouts, "That's enough for the day. Here again tomorrow at first light." He turns to walk away.

"Colonel Ashton," I say in a loud clear voice as he goes. "I'll write to your wife. To Daisy. I assume she doesn't know the price men like these pay for your famous work." The Colonel stops in his tracks. When he turns back, his face is redder than ever, but he speaks with none of the loud rage of a few moments before. Now his words are cold and slow. "Miss Hellings. You will not write to my wife. You will not mention my wife. Ever. If you do," he takes a step closer and speaks quietly, his eyes on mine, "I won't stop at beating that man. I'll turn him out. He'll be finished. Do you think he has another chance of work once I've told the entire region that he's a filthy thief?" He points to where Singh has departed. "I'll ruin him. And you will not be able to do a thing about it." He walks away. The blood is pounding in my ears and I feel I could pass out with impotent rage.

Robert is still standing nearby, in silence, and I turn to him. "Why didn't you back me up? You didn't say anything." He carries on staring after the Colonel. "Robert?" – more loudly now – "Are you listening to me? Why didn't you help me?" I shove him with the flat of my hand.

At last he looks round slowly and speaks, "I... It wouldn't have done any good. He'll keep doing it, whether we stop him this one time or not. There's nothing we can do about it. Like he said, *The Times* wouldn't care. Most of the readers would probably approve. Who can we report him to exactly?"

"That's not the point," I say. "You have to challenge people like that. You can't simply watch it happen."

"Well, I did run over too."

"But left me to pull him off that poor man."

"You always were the faster runner."

I squeeze the bridge of my nose. The men have all left by now and Robert and I are alone on the hillside. "You're not in the army anymore, Robert. You can stand up to him. If we both had, he might have listened. Or shall I get you a white feather?" I stare at him and, after my last remark, he seems to be struggling to speak.

"Don't you fucking… You stupid bloody woman. You haven't the slightest idea of what you're talking about. What it's like living as a man, what's expected of you. Dressing like a man doesn't make you into one." He stops there; I think he sees how much that hurt. He takes a few steps away towards the tree where Singh had lain and where his blood still spots the dust. He turns back, shouting, "Why do you do that anyway? Why can't you be a normal woman and dress like one? What are you even doing here, Rebecca?"

"What does that have to do with—"

"You'll always be lonely if you act like that."

"Act like what? Standing up for people who can't defend themselves? To bullies?"

"Not that. I mean, always acting the man. It's a bloody rum go, Rebecca, it's not right."

"I'm not acting anything, Robert. I never have," I say coldly. "But I'm sorry you feel that way. Maybe you should act the man next time and I won't have to."

Apparently unable to speak, Robert turns to walk away. I go to follow but he turns and waves me away, before finding his voice again. "Don't. You don't always have to follow me, Rebecca. You're like a bloody puppy. Just go and… Just go."

Follow him? "You followed me to India," I shout after him, "why did you do that?" I rub at my stinging eyes and walk, then run, in the opposite direction from the main camp. More than hurt, I am furious. Furious with Robert. With Ashton. And with the whole day. I run until I crest the hill, kicking up the dust. I must have gone miles by the time I stop by a small pool amongst some trees. I suppose it fills from the little stream that passes through the survey site, but I've never been here before. I sit at its pebbly edge, the round stones quite comfortable under my khaki trousers, and wonder how I can forgive Robert. His words are still turning over in my mind. I don't play the man. I don't particularly play the woman either. But why should I? Why should I be silly and stay at home and cook and do whatever other silly things I'm supposed to do? Robert doesn't know what it's like to be expected to be a certain way all the time, and for that simply not to be you. I gave up on dresses and skirts a long time ago but still always get those looks, as people try to work out if I'm making some sort of statement, if there's something wrong with me. Even if I'm a funny-looking sort of a chap. I'd thought Robert understood, for some reason, but of course he doesn't. He's a straightforward man with a narrow mind who's turned out to be a horrid disappointment. I pick up one of the pebbles and hold it in my hands. It's warm and quite smooth. I throw it into the centre of the pool where it makes a loud plop. I throw a few more. Then a really large one that soaks my boots. I don't know why, but that makes me feel a little better. We've had fights like this before, of course. Ours always was a rather intense friendship, and Robert can be very mean when he chooses to be. Feeling myself getting angry again, I start waking and follow the stream until I find a more familiar landscape again, and begin to make my way back home past the site of the beating. I remember the thing that flew from the end of Ashton's crop and search around for it in the dust. It takes some time to find it in the gathering darkness but, when I do, I feel a wave of nausea; it's a razor blade.

After this, all thought of Erica's scheme is set aside as Robert and I barely speak for several days, continuing to work alongside each other but with cold civility. I feel powerless to make any further challenge of Ashton's authority, in case his threat against Singh was in earnest, as I well-believed it to be. Erica asks me what's wrong, but I wave the enquiry away. "It's only Robert being a damned fool."

I focus on the dig and the men, trying to keep my mind off it, and work returns to a kind of stilted normality. I even ask myself why I shouldn't leave India then and there, but I can't, of course, not without him. And I stay.

Over the following days and weeks, the teams set about the hillside with absolute dedication. They are now sullen and cowed in the presence of any Westerners and have started reporting any new finds in pairs, so at least there is a witness to nothing having been stolen. The top layers of earth are mattocked and shovelled away robustly, and soon the men's labours start to open up a far older landscape. Ever watchful, Ashton calls a halt to the brute methods once the first characteristic signs of Bronze Age occupation become visible, at which point trowels, brushes and drawing boards take over. Despite this, the great haste of the digging has already completely decapitated one or two small urn mounds. Ashton is unconcerned, however, believing the bronze items and their style and distribution to be more interesting than their method of burial. I see he has taken to carrying his riding crop with him at all times.

Once the first three feet or so of earth have been removed, like the scraping of a pat of butter with a knife, we can get some idea of what the round-eyed green face was part of. The spring which must have carved out the deep gully is surrounded by at least sixty cremation urns, and who knows how many more must have been borne away by the water as the stream's course has altered in years past.

Robert stares down at the array, each urn site having been staked so the entire spread can be better seen at once, and says, "Doesn't strike me as the best place to bury people – your water source."

Ashton grunts. "Wasn't necessarily their only water source... and anyway, whoever buried their dead here wouldn't have had your notions of hygiene, Baker. And the point you're missing – and of course you would – is that they buried their dead here because the place was important. Water's another boundary, quite apart from being what keeps one alive in this hot fucking place." He looks at Robert with puffy eyes and, pulling out his riding crop and beating the air with it, continues, "It's a line between areas of land as well as between here and other places. It moves, it's fluid, it's going where you can't easily follow. It's outside time. Are you capable of following any of this?"

"Oh, forget it," says Robert, but Ashton continues, ignoring him. He walks around the staked area, staring down across the neatly cut and brushed surface and the small wooden sentinels marking the resting places of people so long dead.

"Of course, they drank the water and its boundary symbolism was probably all wrapped up with that." Ashton, warming even more to his theme, quickens his pace and the thrashing of the crop. "What more profound way is there of communing with your ancestors than by drinking water suffused with their death? Their bones? It's worshipping the dead and river cult all wrapped up together." He snaps round towards us. "It would make the ancestors live forever. You've heard of burial practices where bodies are exposed on mountainsides until the bones are completely cleaned and disarticulated by birds and weather, then cast in together in a shared tomb? Well, no, of course you haven't. You've no fucking idea. But it's the same thing, don't you see? Time doesn't run as we think it does today, not in a straight line. Dead relatives, people who happen to be alive now, people who aren't yet born are all part of one greater… thing. Human bodies are a mere…" he waves his hands in frustration as he seeks the right words, "a… temporary…" he thrashes away, "necessity within that thing's life cycle. Once the individual body gives up and stops working, it's rejoined into the communal, greater body and the cycle carries on." Walking away from us, he carries on, the sweat running down his face. "These urns aren't used as pots for the cremation ashes to be held in; they're simply covers *over* the ashes. The ashes must have been placed into the ground, and the urn popped over the top. It's purely a practical step. They wanted the ash to suffuse the land." He clenches his fist. "Didn't want it washing away in the rain."

Robert, speaking to me but just loud enough for Ashton to hear, says, "I struggle to understand the mind that can be so very interested in the dead but so little interested in the living that it's happy to thrash an innocent man to ribbons." I turn and look at him. And Ashton stops quite still, facing away from us. Robert goes on, much more loudly, "And anyway, this is all such tosh! The pots have faces on them, for God's sake. How can he say they weren't interested in individuals? I don't swallow a word of it! All he's found is a few pots and he's written a whole constitution for these people!"

Ashton keeps remarkably cool. He remains facing away from us. "Perhaps. But it's worth thinking about, wouldn't you say? Otherwise what are we doing here? Couldn't putting a face on an urn be a way of someone trying to lay claim to one little bit of individual identity, where he's otherwise utterly insignificant? One fragment of self."

Magsie

The corridor spins as I try to fit the plastic card the receptionist gave me into the slot. Red light. Red light. Try again. Red light. Once more. Green. The door clunks open. I was feeling exhilarated a few minutes ago, but now I must get into a bed. I must. Now. The door closes behind me and I move into the dark room. Where's the light switch? I feel around the walls by the doorway. Nothing. Then a switch. I push it, but nothing happens. I move further into the room. My feet and my knees are aching. I can't do this for much longer. A doorway. Tiled floor. I reach inside. Something cold. Must be a bathroom. Where's the light switch? I find one. Nothing. After getting back out of the bathroom I see there's a sliver of orange light by the door. I reach towards it and find there's a slot like the one outside that let me into the room. Maybe... I push the card into it and the room fills with light. Get to bed. Get to bed. Two steps and I reach it. Turn around one step at a time. Lower myself down. I feel sick. Lean back, slowly, slowly. Right leg up. Left leg up. My God. Lights off.

Rebecca

THE STARS ARE SPINNING SLIGHTLY IN THE DARK sky. After a few days, thank heaven, Robert and I are back on good terms, he having come to my lodgings one morning to apologise. He'd risen early to get me some butter-fried *roti* for my breakfast, bringing them over on a tray with a large mango-coloured flower. I couldn't help but smile, and took some of the food, even though I'd already eaten that morning. He truly seems sorry, especially for calling me rum, even though I say that was hardly the most significant part of our conversation (and almost mean it). And anyway, I've never been able to stay angry with him for long. The return of our former, easy companionship is such a pleasure that it feels like a cool drink after a day in the Indian sun and we spend the evening together up on the hill, having sent the men home hours before. Robert grows talkative as we make our way through a skin of local hooch and I'm tingling with excitement at the thought that today, finally, is the day for the plan that Erica has carefully concocted to swing into action. I can't say that it was easy to get over our awful row, but even before Robert apologised, Erica had convinced me to focus on the bigger issue; Robert was sure, she said, to see sense and to make amends soon enough and it wasn't a thing worth giving up over. She knew, she said, that I loved him too much for that. So when he came, with his *roti* and his flower, it was a happier moment for me than he knew. And now, as the evening wears on, he's becoming more expansive than ever: "I feel as if I'm living... through a veil. There's this life I should be leading. It keeps hinting to me, I brush up against it and we're only parted by the thinnest..." Robert rubs his fingertips together in the air.

I'm here, I imagine saying, *I'm here with you, so take hold of yourself and break through*, but he goes on, "I'm just not myself, Rebecca. I'm sorry if I've been... lashing out a bit. I..." He's silent for a long time, sitting still on the dusty ground. He bends his head and presses his fingers to his temples until the tips are white. I start to speak, but he continues, "But if I were to break through, it would... it would be dangerous. I can't do it. Sometimes, I want so much to throw it all down. Everything's... heightened sometimes and I'm so close to that... I get excited. That music on the beach in Brighton made me feel something, like it wasn't this world anymore and I needn't, I don't know, be in such a funk about things... I felt really, truly alive." He looks down and falls quiet again. With trembling hands, I bend to strike a spark from Robert's tinder box, to light a small fire so far as he thinks, but also, I know, to give the signal to Erica that the time is now.

"Dangerous?" I say, laughing lightly, trying to keep him from descending into one of his black moods again. "You really are quite... well, fully blotto. What are you even talking...? This all has me beaten to a frazzle, I'm afraid." But Robert is looking at me earnestly, his eyes scouring my face for any sign that I've understood him. But this is so unlike our usual conversations I simply don't know what to say. The flames start licking around the few logs I've gathered, dry as parchment, and I watch them for a moment, waiting for Erica to notice and seeking, I suppose, some inspiration as to what exactly Robert might be driving at. I can't believe it possible that these wandering thoughts of his are about me. I look back at him for a while and try, "Sometimes I feel really free up on the hilltops."

"No," he says, more loudly. "It's not that. It's… Oh, hang it. It doesn't matter."

I try to say something sensible through the fog in my mind, with growing worry now, wondering where Erica has got to and suddenly I feel I'm wasting the chance to understand something, an opportunity that might never be repeated, but I have no power to claw my way out of the confusion that is holding me back. How have I got tight so quickly again? And where the hell is Erica? I can feel the carefully laid scheme slipping away and struggle to focus, to keep Robert here with me. "Is it something you've been looking for? A new opening or position or something?" I even wonder if he's thinking of going into the church, if this all has something to with God or at least something or other greater than ourselves, like the bunk these new spiritualists are always talking, amongst the more fashionable set. But then I see the familiar change and, in an instant, Robert is locked in again. We are back to how it has nearly always been when I try to get closer to him. *What have I missed here?* I wonder, when it is clear that the door that was briefly open is now shut again, with him leaning against it. And now, at the worst possible moment, when it seems the chance is already irretrievably lost, Erica chooses to appear.

"Robert!" she cries, seeming distraught, her spectacles askew and even her perfect ringlets in disarray. "A tiger, there's a tiger, you must go quickly, you must get Rebecca home, please, oh! A tiger!" I'm afraid she's laying it on a bit thick and glare at her to try to calm her down a little but no, on she goes, even clawing at her clothes in seeming panic: "Robert, why are you still sitting there? Rebecca's in danger." She clutches at his shoulder and shakes him out of the reverie he's dropped into. But he simply turns a tired gaze her way, saying, "There are no tigers here, Erica, they were hunted out of these parts years ago. Go back to bed."

And Erica, who was so confident in this plan, that he'd leap up and take me home and that, there, in gratitude and terror and in the dark of night, I'd cling to him and turn my frightened face to his and he'd simply have no choice but to kiss me, this same Erica, falters. "But the tiger, I saw him," she shouts, pointing back down the path through the trees.

Robert stands, slowly. "No, you didn't. I promise. Look, I'll walk you both back if you like."

"No," says Erica. "No, I have Harpreet with me, it's… Rebecca…" She peters out. She hadn't expected to be floored by such blind certainty but, now the plan is falling flat, it seems so obvious to me that it could never have worked. Robert is so sensible; he isn't one to be caught up in silly schemes. I'm such a fool. Erica sits down slowly and I can see in the half-light that her mind is whirring on how to redeem the situation; I feel a cold moment of fear as I imagine her dropping the charade and telling him what we've been trying to bring about. I beg her silently to keep the secret.

She does, so in the end and in the strangest of atmospheres, we sit quietly, the two of us, while Robert stands silent and still, gone again into his mind. I pick up the skin, but it's flat and empty, so I drop it to the ground where it makes a soft, airy sigh. Damn. I rub my eyes and lean back against a tree, knowing now that it really is hopeless. *Isn't this how it happens in books, I think, you give the hero the chance, make him see the girl, really see her, for the first time, and the rest is sweetness and light?* But no. Here we've done our level best to bring it about and Robert is still his stony, untouchable, beautiful self.

Almost in despair, I thump quietly at the tree I'm leaning on with the back of my head, cursing myself and Erica, but a sharp snap and muttered curse further up the hill have me looking round wide-eyed, staring into the darkness. "The tiger!" shrieks Erica, I think almost believing now that it's real and, to my shock, Robert sprints headlong into the undergrowth. I shout after him, but, quickly realising that it's useless, give unsteady chase, with Erica still shouting, "Tiger, tiger!" behind me. Worrying that she'll startle the whole village awake, I shout back at her to be quiet and run up the slope where we've been sitting as fast as I can, dashing through trees and clearings. But as I crash over a stump and through a thorny bush, I realise I'm alone in the forest and don't know what it even is that I'm running towards. Robert is here somewhere, I know, but what else is it that's out here... could there really be a tiger? I slow my frantic chase and stand for a moment amongst the shadows and creaks of the dark forest, a pungent sickly smell of some exotic night-time bloom filling the air and strain my ears for any sound of Robert or danger. And then, the whinny of a startled horse in the darkness, followed by the thud of someone landing in the saddle and the sound of horse and rider crashing away at speed through the undergrowth.

I scramble onwards towards the sound, calling for my friend, clawed at by dark branches and struggling on the loose earth before stopping again, in fear that I am becoming terribly, terribly lost. *Take hold of yourself, Rebecca. Breathe. Slow down.* I stand quietly again, listening for a sign of where Robert has gone. And, how wonderful, his laboured breathing comes distantly through the black and I follow my ears until I find him, with his shoulder and cheek against the rough bark of a tree. I reach out and touch him, then slump to the ground nearby, still gulping for air and my head spinning with effort and drink. "Wha…" I gasp, "what was it?"

Robert doesn't reply. He presses his face into the tree and suddenly his back arches and he retches. After a time, it passes and he slides, slowly and shivering, down the trunk to sit on the roots and leaves and scattering insects below. I reach over again and he is cold with sweat. His eyes are closed in pain, his breath only gradually slowing.

"Do you know who that was?" I ask.

After a few seconds Robert replies, "I think… it was the same man from the hill." *The Arab.*

"Did you see him?" I ask.

"No. A shape in the dark. Moonlight… on a gun barrel."

We make our way back without speaking much more and part company when we reach the village. It is clear as anything that there'll be no kiss for me that night, but I expect him at least to walk me to my door, and bid me lock it. But he walks away, his eyes distant and sad.

The family that lives in the parts of the house other than my small room are largely indifferent to my comings and goings even in the daytime, and as I lift the latch and go into the house, I see no-one. Through a second door are my quarters. I lie down, and immediately stand up again and cross to my trunk for water. I still feel tight in my legs and chest after the run through the darkness and shaken almost more by Robert's reaction than by the apparent closeness of the armed Arab – if that's who it was – in the dark. And sorry at the abject failure of a scheme that now seems so tissue thin as to have been doomed from the outset. But these thoughts gradually give way to dead tiredness as I pull off my clothes and lie down again, sipping at the water. Some dribbles down and pools on my bare chest and trickles off as I throw away the empty flask. The sheets are grimy and clinging, turning into hot hands pulling at my naked body as I slowly fall from the room.

I am woken by the rest of the household beginning to stir at first light. I don't much feel like moving. The room is now only semi-dark and a good place to think about what happened the previous evening. I draw up my knees, feeling the roughened soles of my feet snagging slightly on the linen as I do so. After sleep, it is the Arab, more than my hopes for Robert, that fills my mind; who is this man who seems to dog our footsteps and what does he hope to gain? If he's a thief, it would be easy enough for him to outwit us in a landscape he apparently knows much better than we do. He has a rifle anyway; how easy for him to take us by surprise and for all we have. We rarely carry any weapons now that we're more used to the country and know that our excavation and survey sites tend to be safe; and Robert is really quite right that tigers haven't been seen here for a generation. But I decide that I will revisit the policy of going unarmed.

Apart from this practical step I can't see any answers and hunger eventually cuts off my thoughts, so I eat the food left out by the mother of the family, dress and prepare for the day. Finally I unwrap from an oilcloth in the recesses of my trunk a Webley revolver that my uncle insisted I bring along, and strap it about my waist. It doesn't make me feel better. The gun oil and cartridges smell like death.

Robert doesn't mention Erica's tiger or our night-time pursuit when I see him and I turn, gloomily, back to work. Ashton is still blustering around the hillside excavation, but now seemingly uncertain of how to proceed and unwilling to admit it. It is clear that he feels he's missing something. Something important. The new burial site is surely a great find and should have satisfied the scholar in him – if there is one – it's certain, surely, that people at home in England, maybe even on the continent too, will be discussing these finds for years to come. But they don't seem to have assuaged the antiquarian's lust for gold and glory that lurks in Ashton's heart. As Erica said to me once, he's a stout institute of learning and science, with a shrine to pride and gluttony hidden inside.

The walking survey of the hill seems to have served its purpose now and is scarcely worth repeating. The hill that had seemed to be circumscribed by the great linear mound is apparently bare. We could find nothing at its centre or on its sides. The gully with the green face is towards the mound and Ashton is sure it can't have been the focal point of the whole site, all significant features of which he feels certain are contemporaneous. So, with Erica's help, he sets to re-plotting and reassessing the burial sites and mound to see if there are any hitherto unseen pointers towards any hidden epicentre. The orientation of the urns and their distribution are painstakingly analysed, along with humps, gullies and particular views out from the site – to see if there are any possibly significant lines of sight to other hills nearby. Erica suggests they also consider moon and sun positions relative to the burials, but all theories draw blank. Almost in desperation, it seems, Ashton suggests extending the trenches already cut at the new cemetery site, first to the north and east, then to the south and west, but there is no indication that this will help in answering any riddles or in making any discoveries. It seems fairly clear that we've already found the edges of a discrete centre of burial, and when it's explained to them, the men don't look at all pleased with the prospect of several more weeks of hot, fruitless labour.

But on it goes, and there is little for me to do. I spend some time down at the main tents with Erica, who seems more strained and drawn than usual, and is terribly busy repeating her previous analysis of the site for Ashton while at the same time attempting to draft an article on our progress to be transmitted back to London. But she's glad, I think, of some company. She knows of the beating of poor Singh, of course, who is still recovering slowly in the village, but we don't speak of it.

It takes more than one visit before either of us feels able to face a debrief on the failed tiger ploy and even then, Erica approaches the subject by a circuitous route: "You persuaded Robert to come here, didn't you?"

"Yes," I say, "he was being rather aimless at home and I thought it would do him good. And, well," I finish, bleakly, "you know, there were other reasons."

I'm looking through some of her beautiful and intricate line drawings as we speak, but I can see that she glances at me as she says, "Look, Rebecca, the tiger thing—"

I cut her off. "It's fine, please don't talk about it. It didn't work," and then, lying kindly, "it was a good plan, but do let's drop it now, it's never going to happen."

"But how can you say that?" she asks. "That was only our first try, you can't expect it to come off right away."

"It wasn't my first try," I say. "Really, I feel like I've been trying forever, but I can never break through these walls he has, it's pointless. Look, Erica, leave it alone, will you?"

It comes out rather shorter than I'd hoped, and she flushes, saying hotly, "You haven't tried a thing. That night was the first time you'd done more than loiter near to him and hope he'd look your way. It's like watching some… sad schoolgirl."

I'm afraid that stings, rather, and I glare at her. "Well, I didn't ask for your help," I snap. "What is it to you, anyway? And what do you know about it? You're a spinster, and older than me, too. How would you even know what to do?" She's been looking at me with her usual strong gaze, her eyes magnified by her always-clean spectacles, but now she drops her glance to her lap, where I see she's been worrying at the skin of her thumb with a fingernail.

She says something quietly and I think I catch it right, but hope I haven't, or it will mean I've made a horrid blunder. I reach out to take her hand and she doesn't resist as she speaks again, more loudly, "I was in love once, Rebecca. And I'm not too old, maybe it will happen again, but… I'm old enough to know you don't get many chances and that this might be one of yours. I wanted to do what I could, that's all. I'm sorry."

"Please, Erica," I say, "please don't apologise. Never to me. You've been so good to me, I didn't mean… oh, I'm sorry." Soft fool that I am, I'm crying by this point and so desperate to undo the hurt I've caused, it's like a balm when she reaches out and holds me.

After a time she lets me go and smiles. I smile too, awkwardly, and bluster something about having to get back to work – although, as Erica is quite aware, I have nothing to do – and rush out of the tent, crashing over a chair as I go.

The results of the extensions to the cemetery dig are, sadly, as expected. We have now exposed what seems like half a hill of ancient ground surface and the Colonel really is quite at a loss. All the promise of the landscape seems to have died. Even his military order begins to slip and the man looks crumpled, even dirty at times. The men keep a watchful distance from him; curious prey animals near a wounded beast. Work effectively stops.

Robert and I largely leave the Colonel to it until, a week or so after my conversation with Erica, we decide to broach the subject of our inactivity. We make towards the hilltop, where we know Ashton has taken to spending hours of the day but, to our amazement, our path is blocked around ten minutes' walk short of the spot. Two men stand across the way, one holding an old pitchfork and one a wooden club of some sort.

"Look here! What the devil d'you mean by this?" demands Robert, standing up close to the taller of the two.

"Sorry, Huzoor, no letting past."

"Try to stop us if you like. Now get out of the way!"

To my relief, the men quail, perhaps noticing the revolver at my hip. They let us pass. Somewhat disconcerted, we walk on quietly, not sure what can have led Ashton to have the paths guarded.

"Well, this is a queer one," Robert murmurs as we move on through the forest. "Keep your wits about you."

A few minutes further on and nearing the top of the hill we hear the sounds of digging that had been familiar for so many weeks but that had, until then, largely fallen silent across the whole of Saraswathi amid Ashton's hiatus. It is clear that a deep excavation is underway, as only the heads of the men are visible above the edge of a hole perhaps fifteen feet square.

"Hello there!" Robert cries out over the hubbub.

Ashton's face immediately appears, closely followed by the man himself as he scrambles up a ladder to ground level. The head is dusty and the eyes dark hollows, but a fire of excitement is in them again, quite different from the rage that was darkly glimmering before.

"What in God's name are you doing up here?" he demands. "Didn't the men tell you to keep back to the tents?"

"Back to the tents?" says Robert. "Why? I don't see why I should keep anywhere."

Ashton has now marched up to us and stands between us and the new hole.

"It doesn't matter why. This is my site and you're not needed here." The familiar blotches begin to spread again across the man's face. "Clear out. Go and... help Miss Conston. I don't give a damn what you do as long as it's not here." Appearing to control himself a little, Ashton continues, "Look. You two really aren't needed up here just now. Let's speak later on, back down the hill."

Mystified, but little feeling in the mood for pushing the issue, we turn back. We don't see Ashton again that day, or the next. With time on our hands we wander widely, on occasion with Erica, who not only finds that she, too, is slowly becoming freer than before but that Ashton's company whenever she sees him is becoming unbearable. Erica lives with a fisherman's family in a village around a mile south of our main dig and it is while walking back there with her one day that we mention Ashton's curious behaviour on the hilltop.

"Digging? Really? I thought he was still casting around trying to decide what to do," she says. "Did you get a look at any finds or anything?" We say we didn't and Erica follows up with, "Well, aren't you curious?"

"Tolerably," says Robert. "But anyway, it's not worth bothering the old man. Let him keep it a secret if he wants."

But with an inkling of what Erica is suggesting, as I know her a little better than Robert does, I butt in, "We're very curious. Or I am, anyway. What did you have in mind?" Erica stops us outside her home and, telling us to wait where we are, steps quickly inside, emerging a short while later with a small oil lantern and a brown paper parcel that sloshes as she moves.

"What I have in mind," she says, "is waiting until he's gone to sleep and having a little excursion."

We make our way slowly back towards the camp, not wishing to be seen and expecting that Ashton will be snug at home within an hour or so. Sure enough, he emerges from the wooded path to Saraswathi after a short time, which we've spent sitting behind some bushes near to his billet and sharing around Rebecca's flask of brandy. Once Ashton has disappeared from view, we give him thirty minutes or so more to settle in, then move quietly towards the hill, not hearing a peep from the house.

As we move further into the trees, taking nips of drink as we go, Erica motions that we should move away from the main path. It will be straightforward enough, with her knowledge of the geography, to reach the dig site by another route that will probably not be guarded. The way becomes steep and rocky and I have to move gingerly in the gloom, images playing out in my mind of awful, crashing plunges through the black onto jagged stones below us. But with ever-increasing care and quietness, we eventually near the summit which is, by then, deserted. There has clearly been a recent period of quite intense activity, judging by the scuffed-up earth all around the hole itself, and Ashton has evidently pushed hard the few men he brought up here. We creep slowly towards the lip of the hole, hearing not a sound from within or from the dark landscape all around, and by the light of Erica's small lamp, we peer inside.

It is hugely deep. Unnecessarily deep, judging by what we know of the strata at which most finds have been uncovered in this area. It is also, apparently, empty.

"What the devil is the old bird up to?" murmurs Robert. "A grave, do you think? Is he going to put us all out of the way?" then, more hopefully, "Or himself, perhaps."

Seeing now that there is no need for stealth, as there's no-one around, we stand and walk round to the far side of the hole, where the workers have left the ladder by which they evidently climbed in and out, ferrying the hundreds of bucketloads of spoil that must have gone into the heap nearby. Reaching the bottom of the pit, we move around it together, having, as we do, only one light. It seems an ordinary enough hole. Neatsided and cut with some precision, in line with Ashton's usual work, but not quite up to the standard we've seen before. This has been rushed; it must have been excavated over only the last few days. As we grope about, looking for clues, we at last come upon a small cyst in one corner of the flat bottom of the hole. It's of square shape, perhaps two feet by two, and lined to the sides and base with rude flat stones. It appears that a larger stone was laid across the top of the recess formed by the others, which stone now lies to one side. There is no obvious evidence of what was entombed here.

Feeling scarcely more enlightened than we did when we set off, we make our way back down. Erica and Robert fall into close conversation while I walk some little way ahead of them, then, running a few steps to catch up, Erica calls out to me, "Rebecca! Where are you going? Come on, let's all find something more to drink."

We collect a further stock of brandy, this time from Robert's billet, and head for the waterfront to sit on the still-warm stones and muse on what we've seen that evening.

"I can't imagine what might have been in there, or how he would have known, even, to dig in that spot. How could he know? Dash it all, I don't understand it." I go on in this vein for a while, but the others have no better idea than me. Erica wonders if there could have been some visible sign at the surface, but it seems so unlikely. And Robert doesn't offer much apart from suggesting (probably accurately) that he imagines Ashton's riding crop has seen some action during the work.

We make our way through the liquor as the moon rises. We were all screwed tight as we climbed the hill, almost dreading what we might find, and now I think we've all let go with equal abandon. Some of the villagers appear and play on drums and some miraculous sort of stringed instrument as we watch the night sky roll by. Maybe Ashton has solved the mystery. Maybe the dig is over. Giddy with drink, I dance with Robert while Erica claps and whistles. We watch the sun come up.

But at the same time, I can't shake the memory of the Arab. I feel he is here, watching, forming some plan, the substance of which I cannot even dream of, and I have some sense, some clutching fear that I try to subdue with drink, that this will be the last night that I'm happy in India.

Magsie

I TRY TO REMEMBER HOW TO TAKE A FLIGHT. I HAVE a ticket. I have a suitcase. I think I have to check it in' or something. I have the worst head that I've had in a long while. I make my way back to the departures concourse where I came in, having flagged down another little buggy. I must look rough as anything because the driver man asks me if I need the doctor. I shush him and call him a little man. It's too early and my head feels awful.

There are rows and rows of desks. Which is mine? British Airways. There it is. I have now been decanted from the buggy into a wheelchair with a high back and I'm being pushed around by an Indian man. I think he's Indian. He has a turban on. And a beard.

"Are you Indian?" I can't see his face, but he doesn't sound too pleased.

"I'm English. My parents are originally from India, though, if that's what you mean. They moved here forty years ago."

"Yes, of course. Sorry," I say. "My granddaughter is with a boy from Iraq," I say, trying to show I'm not one of those right-wingers, but realising that it comes over pretty lamely, like 'I have a lot of friends who are black'. Even so, somehow my mouth keeps running on: "But he lives here now. He lost his home in the war, that awful one that Blair did with Bush." I think again of the tea bag back in my kitchen and wish a little that it had been something bigger and heavier that I'd dropped, and Tony Blair's real head underneath it. "He came over with his mum, so there's that at least; they've got each other. This country doesn't seem to have given them much of a welcome. The dinner lady in the college canteen said she wouldn't serve him. Said she didn't have to and she wouldn't."

My chauffeur makes a sort of angry harrumphing sound. Maybe I've managed to dig myself out of the hole, but then again, maybe he's harrumphing at me. I decide its safest to purse my lips until we arrive at the desk, where my chauffeur puts my suitcase up onto a conveyor belt. I wave to it as it disappears on its own little journey and my chauffeur smiles. I feel a bit better after that. The lady takes my ticket but doesn't ask for a passport, which is lucky because I don't have one. I panic about that for a moment until she gives me back my ticket and says something about having a good flight.

"Right then." I crane my head round at my friend. "Tally-ho."

All sorts of scanners and things meet me in the next room.

"Please remove laptops and tablets from your bags before placing them in the trays," says someone. Somehow I don't think they mean my beta blockers. Tablet is another word that's been hijacked by young people, I think, and hazily I remember Tim calling his iPad that last night. I feel a bit queasy at the thought of it. And even more queasy when I think of the silver-coloured one I have in my big coat pocket.

Is it really? Surely not. I must have dreamed it. But I pat my pocket slowly and there's a slim, but quite heavy, something in there.

"Bugger and balls," I mutter. "No, no, no." It's not stealing. They obviously didn't want to keep it. What do I do? I look around, trying not to look furtive or like a terrorist or anything. The queue is moving forward. Need to think. But it's too late and I'm being directed by one of the security people towards a big stack of plastic boxes and another conveyor belt. Just going to have to go through and hope. At least it's not in my bag so I don't need to take it out of anywhere to put it in the tray. I put my handbag in there and one of the security men puts it on the belt, and I start to walk towards the scanner thing.

"Coat off, please, madam," says another one. "Put it in a tray over there." Oh, dear. I decide to leave the iPad where it is. Perhaps they won't notice. I can feel sweat forming on my upper lip and in the small of my back. No-one would know it's not really mine, would they? I go through the scanner. It's a big cylinder thing that I'm sure lets the security chap look at my smalls on his little screen. I nod at him and try a wink. No-one suspects a flirty old lady. I don't think it comes off quite as I planned, but never mind. I'm really sweating now, and my leg starts to wobble as I lean on my stick and wait for my coat and handbag to come through. What will they do to me? I saw men with guns earlier. I see a strip search in my mind's eye. They never would. Well, they've already seen it all in the machine, anyway.

"Is this yours, madam?"

My heart pounds so I can hear it in my ears. I turn round. It's my coat she's holding up. Lordy.

"And this."

It's the iPad. Her eyes are accusing. I could deny it. But

she's just taken it out of my pocket. Say someone put it there? But why would they do that? Could I escape in the wheelchair? I imagine leaping... well... getting into it and shouting, "Run!" at the new chap who's come up to push me for the next leg of my journey. *But don't be stupid, Magsie, I think. That wouldn't work. Bluff it out.*

"Yes," I begin. "It was a present from my granddaughter. I use it for…" I can't think of anything to use this for. What have I seen people doing with these things? "…looking young, mostly. And crosswords," I add with a flash of inspiration. "It's an iPad. It's very expensive." OK, Magsie. That'll do, that'll do.

"Good for you, Kirsty." She smiles and hands it over. Kirsty? My God. What's this now? Quickly back in the pocket. Out of sight. Get away, get away. I turn to look for the wheelchair again. My hands are trembling as I reach to grip the arms and lower myself in. I can feel my face turning hot and red and the nausea returning. "Let's go, let's go," I breathe.

"Excuse me, madam." A man's voice this time. I close my eyes. It's all over. Never even got out of the airport, let alone to Scotland. And I need to get there, I must, to stop him doing whatever he's going to do. And by eleven-thirty this very morning – if I don't catch this flight, I might be too late. And now what have you done, you silly old fool? That's what you get for not acting your age, being yourself. And how did you think you'd ever make it that far, anyway, when you've not been out of the village in five years before today? My head feels heavy and starts sagging down onto my chest.

"Is this your handbag?" Oh, thank heaven. I pop my head up again, see my new chauffeur collect my handbag and hang it on the back of the chair, and I finally make it through to the shops, nearly breathless with relief. Now I'm on my way. The buzz of escaping the hideous scanning hall is like being drunk again. My secret makes me feel like a spy. I've duped everyone.

Maybe being an old lady is the perfect cover.

A bit of browsing and being given a free sample of something smelly to wear and I'm at the 'gate'. *But, oh, I think, looking out of the window. Bugger me if that's not a little aeroplane. Where's the jumbo?*

Rebecca

The following day, feeling rather tired and in need of something else to do, Robert and I decide to go out shooting. We saw a particularly fine peacock two days ago while on the main dig site, and we resolved to try to bag it before anyone else does. The locals are canny hunters, and likely to have been aware of the bird for some time. So, without permission, we take Ashton's pair of Holland & Holland fowling guns which he brought over from England, but has scarcely used, and a long Indian black powder muzzleloader. We also decide that Ashton can spare us a couple of diggers to carry our gear, along with food and drink, and we strike out north along the coastline. We think our quarry will keep inland, so we move to the north where it is less densely populated, with the aim of finding a likely looking inlet to follow into the forest. Robert and I hold one each of Ashton's guns and I wear a belt of cartridges. The porters have a further belt and a powder flask, wadding and bullets for the Indian rifle. We don't really anticipate using the rifle for the bird but think we may find some other sport for it during the day.

We spend most of the morning moving up the coastline, thinking of the peacock only but idly. The day is still and the light flat, but bright. I'm reminded of home and autumn shoots and I imagine Robert and me together on our own land as husband and wife, living full and happy. Once again, it's become a fantasy; the hope that Erica kindled has burned low and I'm able to indulge my inner eye with only a duller kind of pain. I seem to see us from outside myself as we walk, as if it's all some play on stage that can't hurt me.

After a time, we reach a stream that leads straight into the interior through darkly shrouding eucalyptus and push on into a more heavily wooded area. The air amongst the trees is turgid and smells somehow of decay, but mercifully it's relatively cool even as it approaches midday, and we cover a number of miles before taking a break. Robert turns to one of the porters and waves his finger at him, indicating he should turn round. From the leather bag the porter is carrying on his back Robert draws a water skin and drinks. He throws the skin back into the bag with a hint of impatience and we both hear the keening wail of the peafowl. Alert again, we press further into the woodland, following the sound and gently climbing uphill as we do so. We decide to split up. I take the left way, where the land opens into a scrubby meadow, and Robert moves to the right, where the trees continue. We quietly direct the porters to load up the long rifle and be ready in case we flush the bird out towards them. The rifle is old and awkward to load but the porters are proficient. They set themselves up under the cover of a tree and wait silently. I close the breach of my shotgun and raise the barrel. Keeping to the edge of the meadow and in shadow as much as I can, I move quietly along the boundary. Once Robert's quiet steps have receded, there is no other sound as I put the stock to my shoulder and sight at the far side of the meadow, where the two barrels seem to ripple through the foliage. There is nothing to fire at, so I walk on, keeping the muzzle of the gun up and ready.

After a few minutes I've made little progress up the long clearing. The undergrowth makes for hard walking but here with my dreams of Robert, I don't mind. I could stay forever, knowing that he's close by and half-believing that he's mine. I know this is as close to happiness as I can be. I step up onto a stump of wood, feeling my heart lifting as my body rises, but the wood splits and twists. I clutch vainly at the branches around me as I fall, slumping onto my right knee, and pain engulfs my leg. Gasping, I look down to where a broken branch has pierced my knee, blood already starting to soak my trousers where my falling weight seems to have driven the sharp wood deep inside. Heat surges up my back and neck, and I feel a violent sickness, unable to scream out, hardly able to breathe. The peacock erupts from the far end of the field. Flying straight, and climbing, it passes me, my gun forgotten, useless. The bird's frantic wingbeats are slowing as it nears the lower end of the clearing and sees the open land before it and the sea beyond, but moments before it reaches the trees, its heart explodes. The rifle bullet crashes through its fragile chest and the blue peacock is stopped still in an instant. Where it had been beating the air and hurling itself forward, it is now profoundly still, seeming to hang for a moment in the air before falling. Even in pain as I am, I'm struck by the awful speed of its end, and the weight of its body hitting the earth as it ends its arc to the ground. I seem almost to lose my conscious mind for a time, and I spend the rest of the day miserably, at times half-awake and wishing the peacock had made the safety of the trees, and at others drifting somehow between knowing Robert is with me and knowing he is gone.

Robert arranges for me to be picked up from the hillside by some men from the camp. They carry me on a stretcher, once the camp doctor has strapped up my leg. He doesn't seem overly concerned by my injury, and is sure that, given time to heal, I'll be walking again soon. I'm not so confident and put his bullishness down to the awful severity of the injuries he has dealt with in the past in France, and the relative insignificance of mine. And when Robert comes to find me later, he's far more concerned with the abilities of the Indian marksman than with my knee. He does inspect it cursorily and calls me a silly clot for having fallen (with which I am inclined to agree).

"That shot… No soldier I've ever met could have done it. Unless it was sheer chance, of course. But the devil looked as calm as you like. He didn't doubt he was going to hit it and there it was, plumb. Dead. I'd like to see him do it again. I've given him a feather as a prize."

Robert wonders some more at this before going off for supper. Some has been brought to me on a tray. Before he goes, he squeezes my hand and promises to be back soon. "It won't be too wretched for you here in your hovel, I promise," he says, and despite everything, I manage a smile. When he's gone, my knee seems to call out for fuel for its repair; I eat heartily and, shortly after, sleep, dreaming of a marksman bearing a ragged feather about like a trophy, and of blood, and pain.

Magsie

WITH A LOT OF HELP FROM A LOVELY STEWARDESS who smells of some sweet perfume I remember from somewhere, I make it out of my wheelchair and onto the steps leading up into the little aeroplane. It does look quite big now I'm close up. The propeller blades are black and seem to bear down on me like the grim reaper's scythe as I pass them slowly on the way up the steps. I try to speed up a little, but I don't think the stewardess notices. The seven o'clock sun is already bright and the white skin of the aeroplane glows against the drab concrete and dirty-looking grass of the airfield.

Once I'm in my seat I shake off the gloom that had descended and look around me. The cabin is very narrow, with two seats on each side and an aisle between them all the way down, broad enough for a slim person to walk but not for two to pass. The stewardess brings me a plastic cup of water and as the coldness of it startles my mouth, I realise this is the first thing I've had to drink all morning. I've been drying out again.

And nothing to eat. Don't they give out food on aeroplanes sometimes? Maybe when we've taken off.

I peer out through the tiny round-cornered window next to my seat. Can't see much. Some sort of wagons moving around. Men in bright yellow jackets. I slide the shutter up and down but stop when a small brown-haired boy in the seat in front looks round at me.

The reaper blades are just behind my seat. Still and silent. Waiting. It's all plastic in here. Even the window, I realise, and I give it a little tap. I can see a magazine poking out of a pocket in the back of the seat in front of me, where the stern child is sitting. I might take a look. I give it a pull, but the pocket's stiff and holds on tightly. I change my grip, manage to get it out, and start to flick through. *High Life*, it's called.

I wake up with a jolt when we land, the magazine forgotten on the floor. A long tunnel is attached to the side of the aeroplane, so I don't have to worry about the steps. When I reach the building, another chauffeur is ready to wheel me through the airport. This time my wheelchair says 'Edinburgh Airport. Where Scotland Meets the World' on the back, so I know I'm in the right place. I'm trundled away to collect my old suitcase, which looks sad and small and battered amongst all the big, shiny wheelie cases sliding round the carousel.

My chauffeur puts it in a little trolley that attaches to the front of my chair, which I think is rather clever. I give him an approving look.

Now that I'm here, I find I can't imagine what I'm going to do. Just wander in and tell George my story? What on earth do I really think that will achieve? He's not going to say 'Ah! The scales have fallen from my eyes!' is he, and let Elspeth marry Aban? Of course he's not, you silly old fool. You might make things ten times worse. He might entrench.

Maybe I should go home. I'm all of a wobble as we leave the reclaim hall and roll through to arrivals. Only one or two welcome parties. Just one person looking excited that I can see, and she's a little girl. The woman standing with her looks taut and grim. Mostly people looking tired. Quite a few drinking coffee. And suddenly I see my opportunity for some real food. Those people have Starbucks cups and even I know that that's a coffee shop that does sandwiches. I shout (a bit too loudly) to my chauffeur to put the brakes on. "Where's Starbucks?"

He wheels me over, protesting that he won't be able to wait with me while I have my breakfast, and then how will I get to the taxis? I tell him that I have a stick and I'll manage. Now run along. The green sign feels like sanctuary when it comes into view from behind a travel agent's kiosk. Bacon and egg sandwich, croissant, an extremely large coffee, water. I'd have had orange juice, but I can't these days. It's no good for my joints. I polish off the food, feel the sugar and fat coursing round my body, repairing the damage I did last night. I can feel energy returning to my old legs and my mind is buzzing like it's been plugged into the grid once I'm a third of the way through the coffee bucket they've given me. That's probably enough of that. Now I can face anything. My plan is a good one. George might not see sense, but I have to try. I have to hope that he will. "Right," I say, rolling up all the wrappings and dirty napkin and looking about for a bin. "It's time to be on my way."

"Excuse me, madam. Might I have a word?"

I crane my neck around, the waste papers still in my hand. He means me. What does he want?

"Hello?" I say, at a loss.

"If you've finished your breakfast, perhaps you could come with me for a moment." It doesn't seem to be a question. He has a soft Scottish accent, fair hair, maybe late twenties or early thirties, and in airport livery. Has the manner of a waiter. Have I won a competition or something? I assure him that I've quite finished. He sees my stick and asks if I'm able to walk a short way or if I'd like him to get me some assistance. I feel quite able to walk after my food but not wanting to slow him down, I agree that a wheelchair might be helpful, if he wouldn't mind. There are some nearby. Before I climb into it, he holds out his hand.

"I'm Colin, by the way. I deal with lost property here at the airport."

Rebecca

THE NEXT DAY, ROBERT DOESN'T COME. NOR THE next. I see no-one but the family, who bring me food and water. I have worked my way through all the books I have with me and after three days of damp heat, still air and walls, I'm getting frantic. As the fourth is dragging to its close, the night quite black outside, Erica walks into my room after a cursory knock, sits on a rough wooden chair by my trunk and looks at me.

"Hello there," she says. I move to stand but quickly reconsider.

"Erica. You didn't need to visit, you're so busy."

"So you didn't get the peacock," she says. "I didn't think you would. I'm glad someone shut it up, though. Damned noisy thing it was." She's about to go on but shouting from outside stops her short. It's a man's voice and one I don't recognise at first, with a tone in it of such anger that I've rarely heard before – perhaps only once or twice in my life. I look at Erica. "What do you suppose that's about?" I begin, but with a dropping sensation in my stomach, I realise whose voice this is; for a moment, as the man must be passing close by my lodging, the words are clear. It is Robert. And the words I hear fill me with alarm: "Where's that damned old fool? Have you seen what he's done to that man?" And, even more violently, "Get out of my way."

"Erica, what on earth is he doing? Is he… but he can't attack the Colonel. We need to stop him."

"No, Rebecca, stop, you're hurt, you can't…"

"Help me up. That stick, there, there by the door, get it for me."

She tries to support me under the left arm and to help me to the door, but the pain through my knee is searing and I stumble and fall, catching myself against the doorpost. I struggle up again, leaning on Erica and shouting at her to move more quickly. With her ringlets bouncing crazily, she does her best to help, with me hopping along beside. Her glasses slip down her nose and fall to the compacted earth floor, but I ignore it and half-lean on, half-drag her as we make our way outside. I can still hear Robert's progress as he marches through the village, apparently towards Ashton's quarters. He's no longer shouting, but one of the diggers whom he's befriended is evidently clutching at him as he goes and trying to avert what he knows might be a disastrous meeting. I can't catch the words, but it's clear what they mean.

"Erica, come on, we need to catch up with him," I urge her, but she's stopped still.

"It's too late," she says, "he's there." There is a long moment, filled only by the sounds of insect life and the distant murmur of the shore, when you might have been forgiven for thinking that no people had ever darkened these shores and that they are just as wild as may be, but then, a shout of fear, rising, cut horribly short by the unmistakeable report of a gun – the black powder boom of the Indian rifle. I feel my fingers digging into Erica's forearm, so hard that I can feel the bones beneath her skin. Robert. There's an awful sound, the worst I've ever heard – someone trying to speak, to scream, but who can only moan and gurgle and bubble. All else is silenced in fear at the sound of the gun, but the waves and that sound going on, on and on, and no-one helping him. Erica has become useless, dropped onto her rump on the floor and pressing her knuckles to her mouth in a cartoon image of terror. Somehow, I find myself standing, then walking like a drunk, half-dragging one foot behind and running in the best way I can towards Ashton's lodgings. I can't hear the dreadful sound any longer and I pray, even as I try to run, that it's only because the world has erupted into shouts and chatter, and that poor Robert is still alive, still fighting, but I can barely hold onto the hope as I drag and claw and heave my way onwards. And, at last, there he is on the ground, one hand moving slowly, the eyes wide and pleading reflected in the moonlight, white shirt black with blood and more spreading across the dusty earth. Robert is nowhere to be seen... it is Ashton. I wish I could pass out from the pain, miss it all as the men from the site come to their senses and run to his aid, as they lift him and blood seems to pour out of his body and onto the ground as if from a hose, a dark glistening flow of it as they carry him away, leaving a trail where they go, wet black on the ground and reflecting the bone-coloured moon.

It must only be moments, but it feels like days before anyone comes to help me as I lie, spent, in the path. It is Singh in the end who, with a fellow of his, lifts me and takes me home, even as I struggle with them and call out for Robert. Where is he? Why doesn't he come? Erica is where I'd left her, but when I come into view it shakes her from her stupor and she stands, to dash across. "Rebecca, what happened?"

"I don't know, I don't know," I cry. "Ashton's shot. And Robert. I can't find Robert." Erica runs past me and away to where Ashton fell, but is soon back. Before she speaks, Erica ushers away the men who've helped me and are now hovering outside, wearing worried looks. She says, seeming to have gathered some of the self-control that departed her earlier on, "Look." She pauses.

"What?" I say. "What is it?"

She frowns at me. "This isn't easy, Rebecca."

As she often does, she squeezes the bridge of her nose between her finger and thumb, and I almost shout, "Please, Erica. Please tell me what happened. Where's Robert?"

"Robert's gone," she says. "Quite gone. It doesn't... well, it doesn't look good. He went in there, you heard him, all storming and shouting. And now... this. The doctor's with Ashton now, but, there's blood everywhere, I don't see how anyone can live through that."

I am incredulous. "It wasn't Robert, Erica, how could it be him? You know it wasn't him," and, with a flash of inspiration and gripping her arm again, "you heard the shot – that was that old Indian gun, I'd swear it, why would he use that?"

Erica snatches my hand from her arm. "You're hurting me. And what do you mean? You're raving, you can't tell the sound of one gun from another... it's... but..." She stops, breathes deeply and controls herself. "No, you're right, I don't believe it was Robert either. But it really does look awful. What was he thinking, to have bolted like that..." She pushes her glasses back up her nose – dusty as they are now, she must barely be able to see – and she gives me a queer look as she goes on. "They're saying there was another man, too, in strange dress. You remember the man Harpreet warned us about, God it makes you shiver to think of it, that he might have been lurking there..."

We talk it over for hours but can make neither head nor tail of it. All I know is that Robert would never have done this – never – but the fool has somehow implicated himself. If it weren't for this damned knee I'd be after him like a shot, but as it is, we only talk ourselves into a kind of exhaustion, until it seems that all we can do is stare at the walls and wait for morning. Erica starts speaking again, slowly. She tells me that she came to see me that day with other news. It has become clear since I've been bedridden what Ashton has been digging for, and found, up on the hill. A short while after we three investigated and Robert and I took our somewhat ill-fated shooting trip, Ashton, who it seemed had been biding his time before his great reveal, had gathered the entire camp to announce that the mystery of the hill was cracked wide open. The burials beneath their urns all pointed to one focal point that he, Ashton, had discovered. An incredible find. A monumental find. He had discovered the face of a god. A god unknown to history or to archaeology. A god made from gold.

"That little cyst we found, up on the hill in that great hole, you remember?"

"Yes, of course."

"Well, it hid a golden mask, dome-shaped," she speaks in a soft voice, cradling an invisible treasure in her hands and with a mist in her eyes that, for a moment, makes me wonder if the gold sings to her too. She goes on, "It had lain in there, looking up at the sky through feet of stone and earth, for thousands of years. Think of it. It's… But that's when he really got bad, they're saying, Ashton, somehow he knew something was there and he… well, you know what he's like with the men, and that damned crop. And when he finally got the thing, he kept it secret, all to himself, for days, hidden away there in the house. It was only yesterday, while you were stuck in here, that he showed us all." Erica describes the moment when, after those few days communing privately with the ancient presence, Ashton had pulled it out before the crowd and held it aloft, scattering the blistering sun.

"So, it seems he was right all along," Erica says. "Not such a fool after all."

The next day, I feel stronger and make it out of my bed with the aid of a crutch. I know – know – that Robert can have had nothing to do with Ashton's shooting, except perhaps as a witness, but the rumours persist that he must have done it, or at least been in cahoots with the stranger – or why would he have run?

I know him better than that. Better than anyone, surely. In all the years since I met him, there was never anything to suggest that he could do something like this. I'm clear, and tell everyone I speak to, that Robert must have chased after the man and must still be in pursuit. He was a soldier; he would still feel that sense of duty towards a superior officer, whatever the man's character. And what could be his motive for murder? He doesn't need money. He's not a madman.

In deepest frustration I rest as much as I can over the next days. I'm desperate to get out on the road and after Robert, but there's nothing I can do with this wretched injury and it seems to me that my best option is to gather all the information about the stranger that I can; so far as I can tell, there has so far been little systematic effort to root this out. The local administration has sent a detachment of Indian officers under the supervision of a Lieutenant Avery, a British officer of the Raj, to investigate, but they seem worse than useless. The site of the shooting is examined, of course, and many items from Ashton's rooms are taken away. The men are interviewed, and Erica picks up from her own conversations with them that, more than once, Robert's fury on that evening has been mentioned, as well as the fact that he was seen making for Ashton's lodgings.

"Erica, they can't believe it was him," I almost wail, sick with frustration and inactivity in my rooms. "We have to do something."

I think mostly out of kindness, Erica arranges for some of the diggers to be brought to my billet so I can speak to them myself. I interview each man individually, with Erica in the room to take a note and act as a witness. We also have one of the English students standing by to translate when needed. I naturally suspect the stranger to be the very same man that we had encountered in such curious circumstances throughout the preceding months but feel I must try not to jump to any conclusions.

The interview with Singh (via our translator) is typical:

"He is a good man, a fine man," he says.

"Well, whatever sort of man he is, he did beat you, Mr Singh."

Singh shakes his head. "No, no. He is a fine man."

"Look, the fact is that he beat you and lots of other people. Did anyone ever talk about it? About taking revenge or anything?" He keeps shaking his head. "Was anyone angry? Mr Singh, please, we need to find out who did this. A good man is suspected, and we need to clear his name." Singh's eyes flash for a moment.

"You want to pin it on one of us, the digging men. We didn't do it." He had raised his voice for a moment but now it drops down low again. "We wouldn't have done it. He was a captain for us. We are loyal men, Mrs. You helped me there, on the mountain, and I thank you, it was kind of you, but I can't help you."

He won't say anything more and the other interviews follow more or less the same pattern, and anyway, I feel hopelessly unsuited to the task. Why would these men speak to me, after all? I'm simply one of the Colonel's entourage as far as it seems to them. Erica tries to persuade Harpreet to make discreet enquiries herself, but she refuses, assisting only by continuing her duties as a bodyguard. She is with Erica all the time now, and of course is with both of us at the bay whenever we need a swim. There are many trips these days, not for leisure but out of necessity; the heat seems to have grown since the shooting and is by this time almost intolerable. We swim either first thing in the morning after the long, black, stifling nights or in the evening to ease the passing of another day with no progress towards finding Robert. Or the would-be assassin.

One of the junior archaeologists, Baynes-Smith, has taken over management of the site, which really means taking care of the strongroom, with the valuable finds, the records and other artefacts at the main camp. The excavation is clearly going to be mothballed, at least for the time being, and the trenches are backfilled, their locations having been marked. Baynes-Smith cabled London straightaway after the shooting to request support but so far, nothing has been forthcoming apart from one correspondent from the *Manchester Guardian*, sent from Delhi where he'd been covering the recent political agitations. He finds out no more than we tell him and naturally we keep Robert out of it. I also make no mention of the Arab from the mountain. A few days after I started my interviews and when I'm almost fully mobile again, albeit with a stick, Lieutenant Avery hammers at my door. He's not best pleased that Erica and I have been speaking to the men. Or the journalist.

"You women, keep well out of it. What the hell do you think you're playing at?" Avery is a good-looking man, but quite short and round-shouldered. He wears a thin moustache and greased-down hair that looks like a shiny helmet made from Bakelite. I imagine it would sound hollow if rapped with one's knuckles.

"Well, maybe if you had been investigating a little more actively, we wouldn't have had to take things into our own hands," I snap back.

"How we choose to conduct our investigations is the affair of His Majesty's government. It's a damned silly home rule idea having these blacks here with me trying to investigate, but they are here with the authority of the Raj, unlike you. In fact, they will have buggered things up quite enough already without the help of any damned silly women." He barks it out, his Bakelite head close enough to me that I can smell him. It's early in the morning and for a moment I'm rather stunned by this onslaught. I'm still gathering my thoughts for a riposte when he continues, "I understand there was another British officer here, apart from Colonel Ashton." He consults a notebook. "Lieutenant Baker. Do you know where he is?" I don't feel I can be as reticent with Avery as I was with the newspaper man, so I tell him the whole story of the Arab and Robert's disappearance.

"It must have been that Arab," I say, "and Robert… Lieutenant Baker is trying to capture him. There can be no other explanation."

Avery looks at me closely. "Are you and Lieutenant Baker… involved?" he asks.

"I don't see that that has anything to do with—"

He cuts me off. "It has everything to do with your credibility."

I flush angrily. "Well, we're not involved, as you put it. We're very old friends. And I know Robert's character better than anyone here. He's trying to catch that awful man. And he's doing a damn sight better than you are, I'd wager." Avery smirks at this and asks me to remain in the vicinity for the time being, warning me again not to interfere with his investigation.

"Yes. Thank you. I think I've got it," I say, and shut the door on him.

What to do? I can't sit here, inactive, and wait for this dolt to make progress. But equally, I can't very well carry on with my interviews or I might be arrested myself for, I don't know, obstructing an officer in his duties, or some other ridiculous thing. I resolve to wait until nightfall and to slip out to find Erica. She's been visiting Ashton in his sickbed, something I haven't quite managed to bring myself to do yet, and I find her on her way back to her billet, Harpreet walking a few steps behind.

"Erica," I call in a low voice. They both look round. "It's all right, Harpreet, you can go," I say. "I can look after us." I pat my revolver. Harpreet looks doubtfully at Erica, who waves her away. When Harpreet is out of earshot, I report my conversation with Avery.

"He's told me I can't leave. But he's never going to find that Arab, or Robert. You can tell."

Erica nods slowly and says, "Well, they do seem… rather relaxed about it all. But surely we should leave it in their hands now. And if you've been told to keep out of it…"

"Please, Erica, we need to, I don't know, we need to get after them. Robert can't have gone far."

"It's been days and days," she says. "He could be anywhere by now. Let's—"

I cut her off again. She clearly isn't going to help. "All right, all right. If you don't want to do anything about it," I shrug, "well, I'll walk you home, I suppose."

"Rebecca," she says, taking my hand, "this is serious. It's not some silliness with a made-up tiger. I know you love him, but the authorities are involved now; why not let them take care of it? I don't want… You're going to get in trouble."

I ignore her and she drops the issue, shaking her head, and we walk the rest of the way in silence. I leave her at her lodging and return to the village. I'm going to have to do this alone, and that makes it feel twenty times harder. Why won't Erica help? I half-turn back towards her little house, but realise it's no use thinking that way. I have to get on with it. And if I'm going to go, it has to be now, before Avery can intervene. I let myself quietly into my rooms and begin to prepare a small bag. I'll have to travel light, so I pull out a canvas knapsack from my trunk and load it with as little clothing as I think I can get away with, some money and a handful of ammunition; I hope I still have it whenever this adventure ends. These few things will have to do until then, and I know the first night will be the hardest.

I'm packed and ready, but my head is spinning. How has this all happened? How have I come to be creeping out, armed and under cover of darkness, if not on the wrong side of the law, at least at its edge? In that moment I almost falter but I remember Robert. He needs me now, more than he ever has. I must help him. I have no choice.

It is by now quite dark and quiet, save for the sound of insects. The night is far cooler than the day, but the air is still close and my shirt clings to my back. The pack seems absurdly heavy for the few things I'd put in it. Mostly, I suppose, it's the heavy water skin that not only weighs me down but sloshes alarmingly as I move. I close the door and stand before the house, my heart racing. I could go back inside. Go to bed. But in the end, my feet start moving almost before I realise I've made a decision. I set off.

Of course, I have no idea in which direction the Arab and Robert might have fled, but I select the main road north along the coast as the most likely. In the other direction, past our swimming bay, is nothing but wilderness, but this route leads up by the sea to Ashkara, the nearest port of any significance, and I feel it's a likelier destination, though I know I could be dead wrong. Wilderness and mountains might be the perfect escape route for a would-be murderer, but I have to make a choice and commit to it.

I make fairly swift progress along the road out of the village and towards the next, which is larger. My boots are comfortable and the path easy underfoot. I only curse my knee, that still throbs, and the stick I'm having to use. I'm lucky that there is a moon tonight as without it, this route through the trees would have been black as pitch, and I dare not risk a lamp. I see neither Avery nor his men, but one or two locals about their night-time business.

When I reach the next village, I'd guess it's somewhere near to four or five in the morning. By now, I have to rest or fall down, but asking for help or somewhere to stay is out of the question; I would too easily be tracked by Avery, should he decide to start a hunt. So instead, I find a large storage hut, filled with some sort of crop ready for processing. There is a huge bladed wheel, mounted on a platform in the centre of the room, rusted and dark with age, black oil seeping from its bearings, crusted with God knows what. I creep around it and further into the room. The crop, whatever it is, is hard and sticklike, and sharp where it has been cut. It will scarcely serve as bedding, but it could shield me from sight if I can find somewhere to tuck myself away. But there's no space around the bales; they're packed in tight and moving them is impossible. Each would take two men to lift. The sun is now coming up fast and I have no time to try to find another hiding place, so in the end I have to sit behind the machine, my back against the stone platform on which it sits. If my luck holds, no-one will need to use it today. Propping my head against a wooden post, after a time I drift into an uneasy sleep.

A rattle of wood. My eyes are open in an instant. I look blearily around and, after a moment, recognise where I am. The door to my hiding place is being pushed open. Good grief, what can I do? I shrink down as small as I can behind the machine, my breath sounding in my ears like a steam locomotive, much as I try to quiet it. After a few seconds I hear panting close at hand and a dog's head pops round the corner. Mercifully, it seems rather a slow dog, and rather than growling or barking, it merely sniffs at my head and the hand that lies closest to it. I silently plead with it to leave me alone, find something else to investigate, straining desperately to hear whether its master has come with it to the outbuilding. But I can hear nothing that suggests he has, and I let out my breath.

"Christ above," I murmur to the dog, "you had to come exploring today, did you?"

I stroke its head and the dog lies down next to me. The stone at my back is cool and the air itself seems much milder today. With the dog's warmth against my thigh I even feel a little less alone. Maybe Ashton was right about man's best friend after all.

I watch the sunlight move across the floor, hear a few people moving around and talking outside, but no-one comes in to disturb me. My stomach, though, churns more and more as the day wears on. I packed a little food, but I need to ration it, so I pick at some of the bales around me to see if the plants are edible, and nibble at one of them, but it tastes bitter and I daren't risk having more. Gradually, my thirst becomes even more pressing than the hunger, but as I reach for my pack my stomach turns to lead as I realise it is sodden. In panic, I pull it open and grab the water skin. A steady trickle runs down its side where it has been punctured. *But how?* I scream in my head. I root about. The razor blade. I'd kept it in case I'd ever needed it as evidence against Ashton, hidden in my bag.

In the rush last night, I'd completely forgotten it and it must have somehow found the edge of the skin when I put my pack down. Even from his sickbed, it seems that Ashton's hand is reaching for me to prevent my flight.

I manage to salvage a little of the water, but as the hours grind by, I become as thirsty as I've ever been. I try to sleep and manage to drift off for a while, try to distract myself by watching a bird that flies in and up to the rafters, its beak full of lacy insects. I move around on the floor, trying to ease my knee, and at one stage I can't bear but risk standing for a short while. I feel that I'm almost at the edge of my sanity when the light finally begins to fade.

"I think we can risk it," I tell the dog in a whisper. I shoulder my pack and creep through the doorway, but as I do so, the dog bounds past me and sends the door clattering on its hinges. I shrink in terror against the wood, but no-one comes. I wait, listening to my breath, trying to slow it down. Still nothing happens, so I step out from the darkness of the hut into the twilight outside. My tongue feels foreign, thick and dry, like cured meat, and I start walking quickly, keeping my head down. I've wrapped a shawl around it to conceal my pink and freckly face as far as I can, but my dress is hardly typical. Something I failed to plan for in my haste. And then, joy of joys, near to the building where I sheltered, I find a well. There are one or two people walking in the middle distance, but they seem uninterested in me, so I pull up a bucket and drink most of it off. My cracked tongue is at once my own again. I could laugh with pleasure but, controlling myself, I set down the bucket quietly. Fortunately, my water skin was punctured near one end, so I fill it and carefully pack it with the rent uppermost. It will have to do.

If I can get to Ashkara I can hide amongst the crowds and start making real enquiries. I know I will find Robert; I only have to keep my head and work at the problem. *One step at a time*, I tell myself, but my hands are shaking and faint lights dance in my vision; I'm not going to get far without food. The dog is roaming around the place, never too far from my side, and I imagine how readily it probably finds scraps out here. Life is harder for a human with a delicate stomach but, moving stealthily around the village, avoiding sounds of conversation or any light, I eventually find some mangoes. I fill my pockets and speed off as silently as I can. When I eat in the shadow of a stone wall, the flesh is as sweet as anything I've ever tasted. Mentally apologising to the person whose crop I've stolen, I push off from the wall, taking the weight on my stick, and set off again. At last, I feel ready for the long night's march ahead.

A dark road. I can hear the sea, distant but clear. There are so many stars and they seem to light my way to Robert, to a time when all of this is resolved and happy. To a life we might at last enjoy.

I feel a heavy hand on my shoulder.

Magsie

SUDDENLY MY INSIDES, THAT HAD BEEN ALL WARM and content and full of Starbucks' finest offerings, are a whirlpool. Colin's pushing me along swiftly, perhaps so I can't leap out and run for it, like a gangster from a moving car in one of those American mafia films. He keeps up a stream of chit-chat while he walks, and I feel it's perverse to natter away like this. How can you think I want to discuss the cafes in this airport with you when I know you know about the iPad? I haven't lost anything, so what else can it be? I need to get away from here. I need to get to George's house, what's the time, what's the time? But we pull up outside a white door, tucked in at one corner of the domestic arrivals hall and Colin moves round me to open it. I look around for an escape route while he's busy. I'd have to leave my case. But he's back before I have a chance. I glance back at the concourse, how close I was to freedom and completing this mission I've given myself that now seems so exhausting, as he wheels me towards a scuffed white desk. I see there's a key in the door, but he doesn't close it. The floor is covered in grubby carpet tiles, coming up in places. On the desk is a computer with a big monitor. There's a cat-o'-nine-tails of black wires hanging down from the back of it and trailing along the floor before disappearing under the desk.

"Here we go. Now, I'll just close the door." I listen for the key turning, but to my relief, it doesn't. "I expect you're wondering why you're here. Don't worry," he says, and I realise my silence and probably my face are giving me away as panicking something rotten. "I'm sure we can get this all settled. Do you mind giving me your name?" He's settled behind the computer with its tail and has a pen in his hand. *You don't know who I am then.*

"I don't think you need that, do you?" I say. I'd hoped to sound like a gruff and hardened Steve McQueen, but it comes out more like Charles Hawtrey.

"Oh. Well, no, if you'd rather not give it." He puts the pen down. "I asked you to drop in" – Drop in? I'm not here for a cup of tea – "so we could check something with you. My colleague in Gatwick called me because he'd had a girl in his lost property office asking if her iPad had been handed in. It's a silver one with the name 'Kirsty' engraved on the back. To be honest, he wouldn't normally have called me, but Kirsty's the daughter of Gatwick's Chief Executive, so we wanted to see if we could track it down. We think Kirsty may have left it at the Bloc hotel and the staff there confirmed it. They also said that it had been collected by an ol… By someone matching your description." He looks at me. I look at him. "Do you know anything about this, Mrs…?"

"I'm not falling for that one," I say.

"OK," says Colin. "If you have the iPad, it would be good if you could just give it back. Then you'd be free to go on with your day and I could go and collect my brownie points."

I look at him. *Hand it over and you're admitting it*, I tell myself. As if he'd let me go after that. Oh, yes, tell them you'd also lost your own silver iPad and picked up the wrong one by mistake. Ridiculous. Why would anyone believe an old lady like me would even have an iPad, look at my old case, how could I even afford it? I don't know what it costs, but Tim seemed to think they're very valuable. A thousand pounds at least or I'm a Dutchman. My heart's still going like the clappers and I'm still looking at Colin and he turns his eyes to a poster of a volcano on the wall. Over the picture it says 'Lanzarote' in day-glo purple lettering.

"Well, let's think about it for a minute," he says, after a while. And more slowly, "We wouldn't want to have to involve the police."

"Bugger it," I say under my breath.

He looks at me for a bit, maybe to see if I'm going to say something more, then says cheerily (the sod), "Let's have a cup of tea."

He turns away to a small cabinet in the corner with a plastic kettle on top. There are a couple of mugs and some white china pots with creamer, sugar and stirrers. Now I think about it, the place is full of the stale smell of instant coffee. My knees scream as I get to my feet more quickly than I have done in five years, hoisting myself up with my stick in one hand and my other on the flimsy arm of my plastic seat. The end of my stick slides over the carpet tiles at first but holds firm against the edge of the desk amongst the mess of cables. It's one short step to the door. I snatch the key out of the lock and pull it open with one hand and swing my stick to plunge through the opening, but I feel the loose base catch on something. As I glance back, I see Colin leaping across the desk towards his monitor, shouting as it starts to tumble backwards to the floor. I hear the sound of a heavy object smashing into carpet tiles laid thinly over concrete as I slam the door shut and turn the key in the lock. I'm sorry, Colin, but this is too important for me to be held up by you. It must be a good door, because after a moment or two, when I assume Colin realises what has happened to him, I hear hammering and shouting but quite quietly. I look around to see if anyone has seen what I'm doing. No-one has. They're all still greeting people at arrivals or drinking coffee. My hands are shaking like a blancmange as I put the key in my pocket and start to make my way as quickly as I can away from the office towards the exit and, I pray, a taxi. Ah, youth, youth, I can feel it in me again with the adrenaline, a bit of the real me breaking through the old body again and really living. But then I come back down to earth – I don't have my suitcase. "Sod," I say out loud. *Keep walking, Magsie.* I do have my handbag. And I still have the bloody iPad.

Rebecca

There is a thud and the hand is gone. I stay rooted to the spot, desperate to turn but yet more desperate not to see what terror is behind me in the dark. It lasts only a moment, perhaps a fraction of a second, and I pull out my revolver.

"Who's there?"

A man is lying in the road, his head a mass of darkness and too large. It looks as if it has been broken open and spilled over the dusty ground; it's horrifying. What has happened to the poor fellow? I stare around me wildly. There is someone else here.

"Show yourself," I say, in a low but urgent voice. I cock the revolver, the hammer making a small, hard snick in the silence of the night, and the sound of it seems to draw a figure out from the deeper dark of the undergrowth, where it must have stolen after dispatching the man on the ground. It moves towards me, the long silhouette of something by its side; a stick? A gun? I open my mouth to speak again, but no sound comes out. I raise the pistol. The figure speaks.

"He was take," it says, "to soldier sahib."

I look back at the fallen man. It's hard to tell in the gloom, but is that a red soldier's jacket?

"I coming you... this..." The figure seems to signal back towards the village. Suddenly, I know the voice.

"Harpreet?" Lowering the gun, I move towards her. "Harpreet, is it you?"

"We going," she doesn't seem to know what to call me, and finishes, "lady."

She points to the soldier and seems agitated, as if fearful of him.

"We must try to help him, Harpreet," I say, and go towards the body. *Or even hide him*, I think, my mind spinning at the thought that this man has been killed, if not by me then at least, perhaps, for me. How did this get out of hand so quickly? But as I bend down, Harpreet pulls at my bag, tugging me backwards and almost off my feet. She's speaking fast and low. I think I catch the word 'alive' and even as she says it, the man moves. How could he move? With such a wound? I feel sick at the thought, but in panic, I no longer resist Harpreet's frantic heaving at me and we run for cover into the black of the woods.

When we're well-hidden, I look back and the man is sitting up. I stare in wonder. He reaches up and, with both hands, seems to reassemble his head, winding something round and round. Relief washes over me. It wasn't his head that was broken, but his turban. I look at Harpreet and she seems to be signalling that she had struck him low on the back of the head with her rifle-butt. She mimes someone slumping, unconscious, to the floor. Despite everything, I start to giggle – I think partly from relief – and have to press my face into my bag to keep from bursting out and alerting the soldier, as doubtless he is, who is by now upright and rushing back towards the village, presumably for reinforcements. I fear I may have become of yet more interest to Lieutenant Bakelite.

Harpreet and I move as quickly as we can away from the site of our near discovery. When we feel we must be out of sight by anyone from the outlying farms and buildings, we risk rejoining the road and begin to make better headway. It feels wonderful to have someone with me, even someone I can barely talk to. But as we hurry on through the night, I begin to worry about the risk Harpreet is taking in helping me. If the consequences for me, an Englishwoman, of flouting Lieutenant Avery's commands might be severe, how much worse would they be for Harpreet, who has not only assisted me but struck one of Avery's men? When we stop for water and to catch our breath after an hour or so, I try to convince her to leave.

"Harpreet, thank you." I try to press her hands, but she pulls them away. "Thank you for helping me, but you simply must go." She looks at me blankly. I point back down the road we have come. "You've already done too much. Please." I swing my bag from my shoulder and take out a few rupees. Harpreet puts them into her pocket, lowering her eyes for a moment in what I take to be thanks but remains impassively standing in the road. She seems not to expect payment but nor is she fool enough to refuse it. This is hopeless. Try as I might, I either cannot make her understand or cannot persuade her – I suspect the latter – so when I repack my knapsack and make ready to leave, so does she. I must look at her with such wonder that she understands that I don't know why she is helping me, why she is taking such risks. She frowns for a moment and says, "This is bad man. We are stopping him."

For her daughter, I realise at once. Her child who was lost, all those years ago, and this other child, who is lost now. But

Harpreet's face remains empty. I don't dare reach out to her. Something in her constrains me. I feel, now, that somehow I am helping her as much as the other way around, although my assistance will surely be of lesser use.

Rather than talk about it any further, I have to content myself with a look that I hope conveys some sense of what I feel for her and we press on. We take shelter beneath some trees at first light, but shortly afterwards, Harpreet bids me stay (with the type of firm hand gesturing with which I might have addressed one of my uncle's many pets) and heads off quietly inland. I suppose she has things to do and, feeling exhausted and tense, I don't argue but lie down to rest. I can faintly hear the sea beyond the path and trees and am quickly asleep.

I wake to Harpreet returning. Now, by daylight, I see she is armed as usual with her rifle and a sort of long cudgel that looks black with age. And bouncing at her hip as she walks is a buff-coloured bird, head down, its wings tied in with a leather thong. Even as I see it my stomach groans. Soon Harpreet has a fire going and the smell of roasting meat drives almost every other thought from my head. It is extraordinarily good. I even start to relax a little as I eat, some small part of the tension of last night sliding away into the forest, which swallows it up amongst its snakes and frogs and million bright flowers. We can pass a better day here than in a barn with a too-inquisitive dog.

I try to speak to Harpreet a little more, but it's heavy going and after a time we fall into a companionable silence, she oiling her rifle and me unpacking and repacking my knapsack. As the water skin is empty again, from the slash caused by Ashton's razor blade, I try to make a repair using a small sewing kit that, by some good providence, I have stowed in a pocket. When Harpreet sees what I am doing, she disappears again into the trees to return with some sticky substance gathered in a leaf, which I take to be tree resin. She heats it in the embers of the fire, stirring in this and that drawn from her deep pockets and, taking the skin from me, rubs the substance into the stitches I have made. The thing is sealed up watertight in a jiffy.

When the night comes, we move on again, making the best time that we can along the road. It has dwindled now to little more than a narrow opening through the trees and I become more nervous of the forest and its sounds, so close at hand. Harpreet, though, bustles on quietly, only occasionally stopping to warn me to keep to one side of the path or to tread carefully.

After a few hours of this I'm in a mesmerised state, the moon only occasionally lighting our way as it peers through the thick canopy and much of the time spent in silence and near pitch darkness. My mind is wandering when Harpreet stops dead, half-turning to place her hard hand on my chest. There is something in how she does it that makes me freeze, and my stomach turn over. Somebody is in the forest.

Harpreet pulls me off the road and into the undergrowth. All thought of wild creatures is banished.

"Man," she whispers. "Down." She points ahead through the trees.

We creep forward, Harpreet making no noise but me sounding like a labourer clomping his way to a public house. I try desperately to be quiet, but it's no good. After a moment or two, Harpreet stops me again with her rough hand and signals that she will go on alone. I see that she has somehow, silently, loaded and cocked her rifle and now holds it at the ready. She moves away through the trees.

I hear nothing for some time after that, during which my mind runs through dreadful scenes that might be taking place ahead in the forest, like some melodrama at the talkies. In my mind's eye I see Harpreet shot or, worse, shooting Robert, having taken him for the Arab. I see a startled horse trampling them both in the dark, or Harpreet finding neither Robert nor the Arab but disturbing some terrible beast in the dark and having to fight for her life. I begin to feel sick with my churning imagination and know I must follow, silence be damned.

A whispered, "Man. Being down in… tree," startles me even as I take my first step. Harpreet has returned and is beside me. How does she move so? She guides me, step by step, to a hidden vantage point and there, in a lower part of the forest where the hillside falls steeply towards an inlet from the sea, is a man. I recognise him. Not Robert, but the Colonel's attacker. We could capture him now. Two of us, both armed. It would be easy. And we could find Robert and we'd be safe again, at last.

But there is no child with him. Where is the girl, if he has taken her? I look quickly at Harpreet in the moonlight and start at the sight. Her normally blank face is afire with such loathing as I've never seen. Pain and torment, her toothless jaw set hard and small beneath her wrinkled cheeks.

"Harpreet," I whisper, "we can grab him." I try to mime clutching at him with my hands. "Take him to the British officer." But the woman is beyond hearing me.

"You seeing," I think she is saying, "you seeing." She looks at me, wide into my eyes, and back at him. She seems to want me to see, to experience what she feels, to understand what this man means to her. Enthralled, I turn to look at him as he sits on the ground, his horse tethered nearby, with the remains of a fire on which he's cooked some small supper. He is slumped over slightly, his head hanging and one hand rubbing the dark hair on his head. Could he be weeping? We are too far, I can't tell.

I look back at Harpreet and catch my breath as I realise she is hunched over her rifle, still and silent and, as her finger slowly squeezes the trigger, counting out the last moments of this man's life.

Before I know what I'm doing I scream, "Harpreet!" and throw myself towards her, knocking the gun barrel sideways even as she fires. Flame and smoke blaze from the muzzle, blinding me in the darkness. I flail at Harpreet, not thinking of anything but murder and how I might stop it, then all becomes black.

When I come to, the sun is low in the sky and my head throbs. I reach back gingerly, and it feels mushy to the touch and painful. My vision swims but I see Harpreet standing, ready to leave. She looks at me struggling to rise, grunts, and moves away into the gloomy forest.

Later, after some water and food that, thankfully, she left me, I feel my strength returning a little. I stand and look around me. It's so different by daylight, but it must be the same spot we were in the night before. There are the remains of the Arab's fire; there some droppings from his horse. But no other sign of man nor beast. So she missed. He must have fled at her first shot and then she'd had to deal with me. The supposed comrade who had possibly ruined her only chance at even this wild and random sort of vengeance. Had I been right to do as I did? I don't know. But I can't regret saving a man's life, whoever he is. Nonetheless, I am now on my own in this great forest, surrounded by God knows what creatures and men, the sea on my left, mountains to my right, little idea of where I am heading and still less of what I'll find there. Robert? I hope so, with everything I have.

But hoping won't do much. Feet, Rebecca, that's what'll get you there. Come on, my girl. I heave myself up, pack up and am ready to move again as night starts to fall. At a fork in the path a few hours later, I opt for the left route that runs nearer to the sea than the great ghats, sticking with the plan of making for the port as the most likely route of escape for a fugitive. What is really troubling me again now is lack of supplies. I refilled my water skin during the night at a stream I found tumbling across the path, but without Harpreet to guide me I'm lost as to what I can eat in this jumbling, wild place, and what might kill me. And anyway, the snakes I've seen have rather frightened me off much foraging in the undergrowth. But all that is pushed out of my mind when I hear noises back down the path behind me. It is the unmistakeable sound of men and I steal – despite a prickling of skin at what might be lurking in the dark – in amongst the trees. Before many minutes have passed, the voices become clearer and I can see lantern light.

"You men, look sharp and stop your chatter. There's been someone here." My heart beats more quickly. I know that voice.

"See here, where the leaves are trodden down. This must be whoever it was that made camp back down the path. There aren't many come this way. Well, look at it."

I hardly dare breathe. All I can think of to do is hide and let them pass in the semi-darkness – thank heaven that my drab clothes are relatively easily concealed amongst the leaves. As the soldiers draw level with me, I press myself as far back as I can into the darkness.

Avery is now so close I can hear him breathing, see the faint glow of the lanterns glimmering on his Bakelite head.

"That gunshot was something to do with him, you can be sure of it. Firing in the dead of night. Hunting, you say? No, no, not a chance." He pauses for a while, then continues, "When a man turns against his officer, it's a black thing. It's his neck, you can be damn well sure of that. I'll have that fellow swinging. You men, you'll see what happens." Good heavens.

So he has no doubt it was Robert. I choke back a sob half of rage, half of fear. How can he talk about Robert like that? He doesn't know what happened at Ashton's billet. How could he? No-one does, apart from that Arab.

The voices are growing fainter now and I weigh up my options. Retreat to the village? It would be safer but obviously means failure. I could never find Robert that way and would have to sit and await news, however awful. Or go on – on the heels of these men. To intervene, perhaps, or at the least to hinder. There is only one possible choice, of course. But it means pressing on at once, before I lose them in the forest. Gingerly, taking care not to disturb anything that might be sharing my hiding place, I creep out from the trees and back to the path. There is no sign that I can see that the soldiers have been here. Other than perhaps a faint memory of pomade in the air.

I have to move silently now. Disturb nothing. Be heard by no-one. Not even the spiders and scurrying things in the dark. One foot gently after the other, but with as much speed as I can – the soldiers are making good time. After a while I settle into a rhythm. It's less comfortable than before, when I had the short but solid certainty of Harpreet beside me, but I manage almost to empty my mind of my surroundings and even my purpose, becoming little more than stealthy motion through the trees. Hours pass. From time to time I lose the glimmer of the lanterns ahead and have to quicken my pace. At others I have to slow or even stop as the men pause to rest or, I suppose, make a decision about their path. Whenever I hear him, Avery seems excited – a man on a hunt when he feels the quarry is near, his voice become the baying of a hound.

The light starts to break then, in the most beautiful way. But for me, this is a fearful event. What will the men do – make camp? Search for food? How will I conceal myself? I need desperately to eat, and my water skin, while half-full now, will need to be replenished during the day to come. And the more I think about it, the more likely it seems that the men will disperse when they stop. I need to get closer, so I can keep an eye on all of them. Even one of them looking for water or fruit might be my undoing.

The lanterns are long extinguished and the sun steadily climbing when Avery at last calls a halt. I am perhaps thirty yards away, hidden and silent, and peer at him through the dense leaves and creepers. His face is grey and drawn and his eyes lost in deep sockets. The bluster I heard in the night is still there, but it's somehow ghoulish now I can see him, as if some other thing were inside his spent body, pulling its strings and driving him onward. The men have slumped down wherever they stood when the break was called, but Avery still marches to and fro, boasting again of the end he will make of Robert. The end he would make of any such low criminal. Avery must have driven the men like the wind since the alarm was raised by the man Harpreet had stunned two days ago. They seem to have barely slept. I curse Harpreet silently as it becomes clear that Avery had been on the point of giving up when he heard her gunfire in the night – he hadn't known he was on the right path, but now he seems certain. For the first time, I begin to hope that I was wrong all along about the road Robert took, to wish that he'd headed for the mountains, gone south, anywhere but ahead of this creature with its shiny head and the smell of blood in its flaring snout.

Scarcely able to keep my own eyes open, I watch until all the men, including Avery, are asleep apart from one left on guard. I have a chance here to disrupt the cruel mission. It's a small chance, I know. They won't sleep for long. I guess that Avery will give them no more than an hour's rest before whipping them on once more. If that guard would nod off, or leave for a moment… I wait and pray silently to anyone who might listen. God, Saraswathi, whoever helps will have my eternal gratitude and service. Please, please, I whisper, staring at the drooping head and closing eyes of the young sentry. But something else happens. Rather than drop off to sleep, he straightens up abruptly with a grimace and gathers his things – almost in panic, it seems – and makes off into the forest with the unmistakable, awkward and hurried gait of a man who needs to drop his trousers, and fast. I thank the heavens of all colours. This is it, but I have to move quickly.

Does Avery have a map? Perhaps. Yes, surely he must. I step, oh so quietly, into their small camp. There are around ten men apart from Avery, all armed with rifles and bayonets. Avery himself has a pistol and is slumped with his *sola topi* over his face against the light, his still-perfect hair glimmering gently beneath. Step by cautious step, I pass the men in their various attitudes of sleep and approach him. From the little I know of the man, I imagine he'd keep any maps and other papers to himself, little trusting the native soldiery with anything important. At his side is a leather pouch and I think it the most likely candidate. With infinite care, I draw the pouch away, thanking my stars that he had unstrapped it before settling down to sleep. As I'm straightening up with my prize, Avery groans slightly and the *sola topi* falls to one side. The face it reveals is a boy's, at peace and dreaming. What misguided notions can have brought him here? He stirs again and I freeze to the spot, waiting silently until he's still. Almost without thinking, before I turn to leave, I reach out once more and undo the leather and brass clasp to pull Avery's heavy revolver from its holster. There is a moment, as I stand over him with his own gun in my hand, feeling its bulk and with the smell of oil and powder in my nose, where I imagine how easy it would be to end his pursuit.

But of course it's not in me. I push the pistol into my trousers and make the cover of the trees again a moment before the unfortunate sentry returns. The poor fellow – Avery will not let off lightly a man whose slack work has lost him his papers and gun. But, suspecting nothing and looking happier than before, the man wakes his comrades shortly afterwards and they start to break their meagre camp, readying to push on.

Short minutes later, Avery is shouting in fury as he searches around the spot he slept in for any trace of his effects. I hear his barked orders as I make off into the forest towards the coast. Opening the satchel, I find letters from Avery's commanding officer, one from his mother – that makes me feel a little sorry for him again – and sure enough, a map of this whole area of coast. That, I hope, will at least slow them down for a while. Some few hundred yards short of the sea I come upon a ravine, wooded and steep, with water teeming in its depths, down towards the bright strand beyond the forest. Having pocketed the map, I throw Avery's satchel, its contents and the pistol down into the gorge and head on to the shore.

As luck would have it, on the pristine beach that I find beyond the trees is a small group of fishermen with their boat pulled up onto the sand. They seem to have damaged the craft somehow while at sea and are making some hasty repairs. With a little effort, some rupees and much pointing at the map, I manage to persuade them to take me some little way up the coast towards the port where I must, must find Robert before Avery does. It will probably be wise to keep my distance from the forest road for a while, I think, as I imagine Avery sending sorties out to find the thief, assuming he doesn't simply pin the crime entirely on the poor unfortunate sentry or one of the other men. "Oh, please don't," I murmur out loud.

One of the fishermen looks up at that, enquiringly. "Oh, nothing, nothing," I say, trying to smile. He quickly looks away. I've come upon a fairly surly bunch, it seems. It also strikes me as odd that before we cast off, one of the younger men climbs out of the boat after some muttered conversation and walks away up the beach and into the trees. The oldest fisherman mimes a worm with his finger, explaining, I think, that the youth has been sent to grub for bait. Then the boat begins its slow journey under oar and, once further out, makeshift sail, all the while dancing in the bright chop. Desperate to keep down what little food I've had from the dwindling supplies in my pack, I grip the gunwale and focus on the horizon.

The men seem little concerned to make progress up the coast, instead continuing slowly with their fishing and, it seems, only incidentally moving northwards as they try different spots for a better catch. After some early attempts I realise conversation isn't going to blossom – at least so far as I am concerned – so pass the day lost in silence. I try to shelter from the sun behind the side of the boat, but as it climbs higher in the sky my small patch of shade shrinks further and further until there is nowhere to hide from the punishing white hot glare. Between the baked wood of the boat and the dazzling brightness of the day, I feel I might shrivel up before we make land, but the men chatter on oblivious.

I have drifted into a doze when a great scraping sound tells me that the boat is being dragged through the shallows. The older man is shouting at me to get out, tugging on his grey beard in his frustration. I hold up my hands in apology and leap down into the surf, lending a hand to pull the boat clear of the water and up onto the pebbles and sand. After my sleep the smell of salt and fish is pungent but not enough to detract from my joy at having solid ground beneath my feet once more. I scoop a handful of sand from the scrubby beach and squeeze the sea water from it before dropping the claylike lump back down. The forest has petered out a little here, and there are some sparse buildings a little further along the coast.

"*Bandaragaah?*" I say, trying to repeat a word Harpreet had used when I'd explained to her where I was heading in search of Robert.

The men seem pleased with this and agree that, yes, this is the port. I gather my knapsack and make to set off, giving what thanks I can, but the men quickly gather round. One of them grabs the strap of my bag and the grey bearded one points at the ground in a way that seems emphatically to mean 'stay'. There is no more chatter and they've made a barrier around me, their faces stern. I push the man who's grabbed my knapsack. He stumbles back, falling over a piece of driftwood, giving me a moment to pull out my revolver, but immediately it's dashed from my hand by an oar. Screaming aloud, I shoulder another man who's stepped forward, and manage to break away to run up the gentle sandy slope towards the edge of the settlement. But the men are too fast for me. I shout and struggle with them, fighting with my fists and feet. One of them put his rough fish-scaly hand over my mouth and I bite the flesh, tasting the metal of his blood as it spills into my mouth. The man draws back his hand, screaming a curse at me and strikes me across the face with all his weight. I barely feel it, I am fighting so desperately to get away. But there is no chance. Within a few moments my knapsack has disappeared into the boat, stitched water skin, razor blade, food and all, and my hands are trussed behind my back. Even then, I only stop struggling, screaming, and trying to kick the men and make my escape, when I see a familiar red jacket approaching from the town. A red jacket around a young man with a Bakelite head beneath a clean *sola topi*, shining white in the sun.

"Well done, you fellows," he says, as one of his men translates. And then, more quietly to me, "Natives can always be trusted to sell a fugitive, you know. Keep them poor and hungry and the rest is easy." I want to spit at him, but my mouth is dusty dry save for the fisherman's blood. My head throbs. Even my knee seems to have flared up again to play its part in this most awful of days. I'm suddenly so tired that it takes all my strength to damn and blast Avery for the idiot he is.

"Why are you chasing me?" I go on, when the first flare of my rage is passing. "You know I didn't shoot Ashton. But out here somewhere is the man who did. All I'm doing is—"

He cuts me off. "Yes, Miss Hellings, we know what you're doing. One of my men is still in the infirmary, punch drunk, after your efforts." I open my mouth but shut it again. There's no need to bring Harpreet into this.

"And you've also impeded an officer of the Crown in carrying out his duties. I look forward to you repaying that debt at His Majesty's pleasure."

He looks genuinely thrilled, savouring the thought, as he describes the sentence of years that he will ensure awaits me in England.

"Shame," he goes on, his head on one side, "you might have scrubbed up nicely in better circumstances."

With an appraising look like a farmer checking his stock at a show, he reaches out slowly and pinches my breast with his gloved hand, as the men behind me grip my arms.

"Well, take her up to the fort."

Focus, Rebecca, don't lose control. I try to block out what's happening to me and to keep my mind on what is important – on keeping Robert safe.

"The man you're looking for... the one you need to catch—"

"Yes, we'll find him without your help, don't you concern yourself with that any longer," snaps Avery. "Goodness knows how much time you've already lost us on this wild goose chase, though, the blighter's certainly not anywhere around here." Not here. Well, thank goodness they haven't caught him. So have I come the wrong way after all? I hope desperately that I have. That I've led Avery far away from Robert. I start to speak again, but Avery catches my face and holds it, with his own so close to mine that all I can smell is pomade and his breakfast eggs.

"Hold your tongue, little dear, or I'll give you something to shout about. Maybe you don't need to go up to the fort quite yet."

He reaches down to his crisp white breeches.

But before Avery can do anything more, a shout from the edge of the group startles everyone. The men part slightly and there she is, Harpreet, looking down the barrel of a gun that is pointing directly at Avery's shining head. She is saying something, slowly and loud. One of the men quickly starts to translate while everyone else stands stock still and silent.

"That woman has done nothing. I am the one. I hit your man. With this rifle-butt. I hit him in the dark in the back of the head. You know it wasn't this woman. How could she have done it? He'd already apprehended her." I glance at Avery and he looks rather lost, doubtful for a moment, like a boy out alone and a little frightened, but then his eyes flash again.

"But she stole my map and orders and..." he seems unable to mention the loss of his service revolver, instead finishing, "interfered."

"I stole your map and your orders," says Harpreet, "and your pistol. I sold it. Here are the rupees I got for it."

She throws down a small, heavy bag. Has she been watching all this time? Avery hesitates, looks down at the sand, at me, down again. Finally, without lifting his head, he points at Harpreet and says quietly, "Put her in irons." But the men either don't hear him or ignore the command and they stay rooted to the spot, staring at Harpreet. After a moment's pause, Avery looks up and shrieks, "I said, put her in irons."

The men nearest take a step forward, but Harpreet swings her gun barrel around and there seems no doubt that she would use it. The men stop and Harpreet speaks again, the interpreter carrying on, "Let her go first."

Avery says nothing, so she continues, "Let her go and I'll come with you. I'll put this down and go to the fort." She jerks her head towards the town. This is more than I can take.

"Harpreet, no," I cry, "it's too much. What are you doing?" I start struggling against my bonds again. It seems I don't warrant translation, but Harpreet looks over and says to me directly, "Girl is found, Mrs, was run away to *daadee ma*. Not *badamaash* man in tree doing." The girl, found? I thank heaven for it as Harpreet dismisses me with a wave of her head and continues, to Avery, through the translator, "You don't need this woman. Take her and put her on a ship. Get rid of her. I'm the one you want." At this, Avery seems to shed the little authority that he'd had left. Even his hair seems to lose some of its sheen under the white helmet. This toothless woman has ordered it, and he'll arrest her, and let me go. My hands are untied, my knapsack returned, though not my revolver, and I run to Harpreet, trying to reason with her, to stop her from doing this. But her face is as blank as ever. I try Avery, but he backs away from me, ordering two men to 'get this woman away, and lock that one up'. I'm still pleading as they frogmarch me away to the port, with Harpreet behind me laying down her arms.

But when I reach the open space of the harbour-side with my escort, see the boats, the glittering water, the crumbling stone, the teeming plants and monkeys, the parcels and stevedores, can it be? I squint in the bright sun but there, I'm sure of it, there is Robert in the saddle, looking full of light and energy as I've never seen him before. But strained, searching for something. He doesn't see me and I dare not call out, for fear of giving him away. *Robert, get away, get away,* I will him with all my strength to turn, to leave this place. Avery is only moments behind, bearing his criminal to the fort. *Get away, please, Robert, please.* Tears cloud my view, blurring his shape. I try to brush them away, but my arms are pinned in the tight grip of two men. Robert still hasn't seen me and I can hear Avery's party nearing us. My heart thumps like a wild beast in my chest, straining against its bonds. *Robert, go. Please. Why doesn't he move?* Then, seeing the splash of scarlet and white as Avery enters the open space at the head of his column, with Harpreet in bonds amongst the men, at last Robert spurs his horse. It rears and the soldiers turn as a man. Robert's eyes seem to lock onto Avery's as the horse's hooves clatter again to the rough road and, for a moment, the two men face each other, still and silent across the teeming harbour. Now comes Avery's command to fire.

I hear myself screaming as the horse turns, rifle fire grazing its flank and opening a red line of blood. Its great hindquarters seem to churn in slow motion as Robert kicks his mount to a gallop along the road away from Avery and the flashing smoke and lead. He's going to make it. He must make it. I fight and strain, catching only snatches of his flight. Is it blood? Whose shout of pain? Did I see him fall? *Don't take him from me. Don't take him.*

Magsie

Quarter to eleven. I'm in a cab. Never mind the suitcase. I've got away. Heavens, Simon, if you could see me. What would you think? What would you say? Nothing good, I'd wager. But then, maybe an old lady's allowed a bit of bad behaviour, if the mood takes her. Even though I'm on the move again now, my stomach's like lead as the cab seems to take forever getting away from the concourse at the front of the airport. So many people being picked up, hugging each other, loading cars; get out of the way, I shout at them in my head. As the airport disappears at last, I actually start to feel euphoric; I'm going to make it, I'm going to stop him and get him away from that dreadful Mick, get him to see sense. Who can do that for a son if not his mother? And all the little problems of the last two days seem to recede. I can easily get new clothes and I needed a new suitcase anyway, or at least, that battered old thing was no loss. And Colin will make it out alive, it's no big thing really, just a little story for him to tell his friends, how he was bested by a little old lady that time.

"So," I say to the driver as we pull away, but I peter out a bit. "How's… your day going?" Steady on, Magsie. Don't seem an oddball or he'll be suspicious. He peers at me in the rear-view mirror. The top of his head is shiny, and dark hair is slicked down around the sides. Long ears and a collar that's none too clean but, then, who am I to judge?

"No' bad. It's been long already, though. I'm on from five am." His Scottish accent is calming, somehow. "Hmm," he says, "and this is a delightful turn of events now, to add to oor enjoyment." Our car has rounded a bend to be met by a wall of traffic ahead. "How's yours?"

"Good," I say. "Very good. I'm up here to see my son. He's an ignorant boy, but he's still my son, so there you go."

"I get that," says my new friend. "Ma brother's an ignorant yin too. But I'm stuck wi'im. That's life. What's yours done?"

I think for a moment. "Oh, never mind that." I open my mouth to ask more about his brother, but a blue light glimmers in the mirror and I stop. *It won't be anything to do with you, Magsie.* I keep looking ahead. The light grows and soon it's dancing across the headrests and glinting on the cabbie's polished scalp. He peers round.

"Pollis."

I keep my eyes ahead. The lights get closer. The police car must be crawling along the hard shoulder. A white bonnet creeps into the tail of my vision, where it's fuzzy. I sink a little lower in my seat. The white car stops and I risk a glance. Quick. God. I'm going to be sick. I look around me. Could I get out the far side and escape through the traffic? Don't be stupid. The policeman is motioning at my cabbie to pull off the road.

"Ah, what the fuck?" he asks no-one in particular. He strains across the cab and winds the near side window down. "Have I a light out or something?" he shouts at the white car. Its driver doesn't reply but motions again for the cab to pull over. I look away from the policeman again. Maybe it's the driver they want. Maybe he really does have a broken brake light. I give a little jump as I see a small girl staring in from the car in the next lane out, eyes wide, blue lights flashing in them. I look away, realise my knuckles are white and the clasp of my handbag is digging into my palm as I grip it. A moment later and we're on the hard shoulder, half in the verge of sour yellow grass, drinks cans, crisp packets and long, wet-looking creepers of torn plastic bags. I leap again with fright as someone raps on the window. The policeman is looking in. At me. I hear a muffled voice: "Will you step out of the car, please, madam."

The driver turns fully round to look at me, eyebrows far up his bald head.

"Are you on the run, lass?"

I feel around the door, looking for the handle to open it. I'm suddenly so tired. The policeman knocks again.

"All right. All right," I say. I can feel tears on my face. Stupid old woman. But I have something to do, it's important, and I find I'm saying it out loud. "Why couldn't you let me go?"

The taxi driver is wide-eyed and silent now, and faces are turned towards me in all the stationary cars. Staring. My knees hurt. My hand hurts where I've been using my stick too much. My head hurts from the wine.

"Why couldn't you let me go?" I say again.

The policeman's face has softened a little. I think he's not used to crying old ladies.

"Hey, Mac, can't you give her a break? What'd she do? It can't have been that bad," the cabbie is saying.

The policeman ignores him. "Let's get you to the station." He puts me in the back of the car, hand on head. There's another one in the front, hatless. He glances at me as I put my belt on. I've calmed down a bit now I'm in the car – now the worst has come – but then, forgetting about George for a minute, I wonder what on earth is going to happen to me. Have I seen my house for the last time? Will I be put away? We continue along the hard shoulder and pull off the dual carriageway at the next exit. After twenty minutes or so more we pull through some peeling metal gates into a concrete yard behind what I suppose is the police station. What's the time, what's the time? I can't see a clock anywhere. I'm sat on a chair for a few minutes. Then up again and through to an inner room, where a plain-clothes lady comes and sits with me.

"We don't want to put you in the cells, but you'll need to promise that you'll behave, OK?" she says. "No trying to lock me in here or anything."

They've taken the iPad. They found it straightaway. Should have left it in the back of the taxi when I was fumbling around with the door. Bugger. I have a cup of tea with sugar in a polystyrene cup. The lady police officer tries to talk to me a bit. Where am I from, what did I come up to Scotland for. They've already taken my name, of course. You can't hide that from the police.

"I was only having an adventure," I say. "I don't see that many people now and I went to the pub for the first time in years and I... had a bit too much and... It felt like I was in a dream when I got that thing. That pad. I almost couldn't believe it when I woke up this morning and still had it. And that chap up here in the airport was trying to catch me out but... I didn't hurt him. I only locked him in. He's OK, isn't he?"

Now I'm worried that he got electrocuted or something when that big computer fell off.

"Yes, he's fine. And you can tell my colleagues everything about it when they interview you. Don't worry, it'll be OK, it's just a chat."

At that I'm really sweating again. "Isn't this my interview?"

"Oh no, I'm not a police officer. Jenny," she says, holding out her hand. "Lots of people work in police stations who aren't actually coppers. I help with the admin and sometimes I help with… this sort of thing, too."

She gets me an instant hot chocolate and has one herself. For a sachet – and a sachet in a police station at that – it's not at all bad. She has also brought over some packets of shortbread and I have some of that too. I settle back in my square, faux leather, metal-legged chair a little more and let the sugar do its work. The pain in my knees is subsiding a little.

"Thank you, Jenny," I say. And I mean it. After my initial terror I feel, in a way, better that the police are involved. Things were getting out of hand. Who knows where I might have ended up if they hadn't come along? One thing leading to another. George might have found out I'd arrived in Scotland by seeing me on the news – 'Granny in high speed car chase around Edinburgh' or something. I can see how criminals end up doing it now, the downward spiral. But with a lurch, I think again of my house and I wonder whether I shall see it again. Will they lock me away? I suppose there'd be no bills to pay, at least. But I'd need my photos. And George, what can I do about George? I'm going to have to tell Elspeth, see if she can stop him. It's the last thing I want to burden her with, but there's no choice.

"Look, I need to make a phone call, it's urgent, can I—" I start to say but a door opens behind me and a man comes in. He's wearing a smart suit, but he's pulled his tie down a little and opened his top button. He has ginger hair cut short and an orange glow of stubble about the chin.

"Margaret Brown? This way, please."

"But can I—" I start, but he just says it again a little more firmly, "This way. Please."

We go into an interview room. I don't know if they were going to offer me one, but I say I don't want a solicitor. It was only silliness, but I'll take the consequences, whatever they are.

The orange man says things about theft and false imprisonment. They record what I say on a little tape recorder on the table and write some things down. After a while they have a statement that they read back to me and ask me to sign. It doesn't sound like me; I wouldn't have put it quite like that, but we've been in here for nearly an hour and I'm tired and I sign it. I look at the page after I've done it. There's my signature. Me. What's it doing in this police interview room in Edinburgh?

They ask where I'm staying. Where they can find me if they need to.

"Well, here, I'd have thought. Aren't you going to lock me up?"

He looks at me blankly for a moment, running his hand over his orange chin. "No, Margaret, this is just a caution. Mr Anderson from the airport doesn't seem too traumatised. You did damage some property there, but he's told us that if you agree to pay for it, he'll be content." He looks me in the eye. "But I think an apology would be a good idea too."

"Yes. Of course. I'm so sorry."

"To him," says the orange man.

"Right."

A short while later they tell me I'm free to go. The panic of watching the minutes tick by only increased as George's deadline approached and passed and all I can think of is poor Aban. I need to get to George's house, to try. I think someone might offer me a lift, but I'm pointed at a bus stop a short distance away. My suitcase is apparently still at the airport and I can go and collect it when I apologise to Colin. Or Mr Anderson, as I suppose I should call him. I'm not sure we're on first name terms anymore and I can't say I'm looking forward to seeing him again. Before I leave I have another quick word with Jenny.

Not far from the automatic glass doors of the police station I find the bus stop amongst some thin-looking trees. I realise as I sit down on the bench inside that I haven't really planned the encounter with George. I've been so caught up in all this silly business and the police and everything that I'm not sure now how to go about it. But that's why you're here, Magsie, that's why you've come on this daft great journey. Let's not fall over ourselves now. The bus is an old creaker and grimy, and goes screaming its way along the steep road eastwards. Grey yellow stone under its coat of black soot and the odd patch of red-brick clatter past. I start to feel my eyes close, despite my nerves and the racket. It's warm on here and the seat is old and soft. With a start, I realise someone is shaking my arm.

"Is this your stop? Did you say Clembold Road?"

I look around. All eyes in the bus are turned to me. Even the driver is looking round from his little cabin at the front.

"Is this you, lady?" he shouts down the aisle. Is it? I try to focus my eyes through the glass to see where we are but then, how would I recognise it anyway? I pick up my stick from where it leans against a greasy panel and go to gather up my handbag.

"Shall I help you? I'm getting off here anyway."

"Thank you."

"Is someone meeting you?" the girl asks with a slight frown.

"No. It's OK, I can manage."

Another girl appears. She must have been waiting in the bus stop for her friend to arrive. She takes the few steps towards us until she's standing at my side. She takes my hand. It's Elspeth. Lord. I cling to her like a drowning woman to a buoy.

"Oh, my dear girl. Am I glad to see you."

"Are you all right, Granny?"

"Yes, yes. Don't mind me. It's so lovely to see you," I say, dabbing at my cheeks.

She introduces me to her friend. They're going out to the pub for lunch, but they help me with my things and see me inside the house. George is out, she says. I've missed him. Elspeth doesn't know where he went.

"Not the cricket?" I say.

"Cricket?" she says. "No, why would he be at the cricket? I'm sure he'll be back soon, have a cup of tea, a lie down, I'll be home a bit later on too and we can catch up about… everything."

Alone again, I settle myself on the sofa. I was so desperate to get here, but now I realise that all I can do is wait. The house is Victorian. Heavy, dark stone outside and painted white and airy inside. That's Nastia, that is. Elegant, simple. You wouldn't think it was the home of a racist. No, I can't use that word about him. It sounds so final. He's just someone who needs a bit of re-educating.

After a while, the door goes and I hear keys drop onto the side table in the hall and what sounds like someone shuffling off a jacket.

"George?" I call out, and immediately hear stamping footsteps. He yanks open the door into the living room, bouncing the brass knob off the wall where it cracks the plaster. His head looks beetroot red and even balder than when I saw him last. "Where the fuck have you been?" he shouts.

"What?" I say. "I told you I was coming and you said you'd be off by now. The cricket, you said."

He remembers his lie and falters slightly, but quickly finds his thread again: "I've been to the fucking airport looking for you, thought it would be nice to collect you and there's no-one there. I looked all over."

"Well, I didn't know you'd come to get me," I say, "you hardly seemed very pleased when I phoned, how would I know that's what you'd do?" This isn't a good start, but thank God he's here at least, not off goodness knows where with that horrible Mick.

"Mum," George says, squeezing his eyes closed and rubbing them, "sorry. You're right, you didn't know. But how did you get here from the airport? I guessed you wouldn't… I don't know, I thought you wouldn't be able to manage it. But then," he sinks into a soft cream armchair with mahogany feet, "I guess you did make it all the way up here." He crinkles his eyes at me in apology, the way he used to when he was little.

"It's all right, George." I want to reach out and hold him, touch his arm at least, but he's all the way on the other side of the room and I don't want to push my luck, so I end up sort of patting the arm of the sofa as a proxy for him. Now I'm here, in his territory, I have no idea how to broach the thing. "George," I start, but opt to delay, "do you think I could have a cup of tea? It's been a long old morning already."

"Yeah, of course," he says. Then he calls from the kitchen to ask if I've had any lunch. The hot chocolate and shortbread does feel a long time ago, but I'm not that hungry. Still, better to take what's offered, accept the gift that's given, so we eat sandwiches together and despite myself, I enjoy it. George always was good with food and this is quite something: mozzarella, basil, tomatoes that actually taste of tomatoes. The crusty bread's a little tricky with my false gnashers, but it's worth the effort. He's a normal colour again now, too. Good.

"You know why I'm here," I say. He doesn't look up, keeps his eyes on the last scraps of sandwich he's gathering up. "It's about Elspeth," I say. "You can't stop her, you know, if she wants to be with that boy."

His eyes snap up, and I think I see a hint of the beetroot coming back, but his voice is quite calm. "I'm her father. If I can't tell her what to do, what are you doing up here telling me what I can and can't?"

For a moment, I'm stumped. He has a point. "But George," I say and I see beetroot moving across his face in earnest this time, "the problem is that you're wrong. And I'm right."

Rebecca

London, 1935

As I nudge open the door to our offices, I hear shuffling in the nearest rooms as people register my arrival.

A loud, "Morning!" comes through a slightly ajar and scuffed panelled door at the far right-hand end of the short corridor.

"Morning," I call back, relieved that Ardeau is in already. We share our cramped room and he makes my otherwise mundane working life quite bearable. Ardeau is a clerk and I a junior solicitor now (which still sounds odd when I say it); one of a very few women in the profession.

"Is there any tea?" I ask. The white, half-panelled room that I step into, to Ardeau's cheery smile and bustle, is in a house from the last century near Bedford Row. In the usual style, the names of those practising law within are painted in the archway of the door to the street. Mine is not yet included and I'm trying quietly to persuade the partners that this is not only unfair but bad business; despite the absence of 'Miss R. Hellings' in white paint at the door, we're fairly renowned in the district for having a lady solicitor, and isn't all publicity good? They think not.

As I sip the tea Ardeau has brought in, I wonder how much longer it will take for me to gain this small recognition and somehow that thought carries me back over the past years in faint bewilderment at the journey I've taken since India and the changes wrought in my life since then. Now, work is steady, life dull, my time spent mostly in these rooms, occasionally in the comfortable homes of clients across London and, as little as I can help it, in my own small flat in Ealing.

Ardeau assists me chiefly with managing smaller estates and trusts of one sort or another. I'm regularly astonished by the pots of money lurking in unexpected places and the equally unexpected things people choose to do with them when they die. Choices that lead to wild outbursts, accusations, battles and attacks, in court and otherwise.

Once he has finished pottering about with the tea, Ardeau brings in the morning's post. I leaf through the pile and one letter stands out from the rest. Ardeau has cut the envelope open with his old ivory-handled letter knife but has not pulled out the sheets of handwritten paper. I can see that it was originally sent to me at Uncle's address, but someone has struck that through and forwarded it on here. I suppose it must have been Mr Oughton at the post office, with whom I'd left my details against this eventuality. I pull out the sheets – there are only two – and begin to read:

Rebecca,
I'm so sorry that I've taken this long to write. I didn't know what to say. But I was sure that you knew I had nothing to do with that oaf being shot.

I feel the hairs standing up all over my body and put my tea down with a clatter on the saucer.

"Miss Hellings – are you quite well?" asks Ardeau.

"Yes. Thank you. It's only… I hadn't expected to receive this letter." I put it down for a moment and smile at Ardeau to reassure him. "It's nothing. Don't worry." I want to be able to read this properly without someone watching for my reaction. "Perhaps you could make some more tea?"

> I didn't, of course. If it does need to be said. But I'm not sure I can tell you who did. I can tell you one thing: it wasn't the chap we saw in the mountains. In case you thought it was. But it was dark in there and I can never be certain of what I saw, or whom.
>
> I owe you as much of an explanation as I can give, so here it is. That night, I'd gone to meet Erica. I wanted to talk to her about what we'd seen on the mountain, where Ashton was digging. I wanted to start gathering evidence. Make a log of what the old devil was up to. Thrashing those men. Boys, some of them. If they raised a hand back to him, it would have been their lives. Or as good as. But I couldn't find Erica and as I was heading back to my own lodging, I saw a fellow sitting by a tent, who'd obviously come back from the mountain earlier on after a day's work up there in the secret hole. I tried to speak to him and he could barely stand. His clothes were soaked in blood.

The ink is thick and the words deeply pressed into the page. The lines don't run straight across the page but slope away to the right, more and more so as the text goes on.

> Something in me became blind to all reason on seeing that man, Rebecca. All I could think about was Ashton. I wanted

to give him a taste of his own medicine, that vile bully. See how he liked the crop. You told me that day that I'd been silent, hadn't backed you up, and your words had rankled in me ever since. Now, I think that's partly what drove me to it.

Ashton was in his lodgings, in the dark, when I got there. I could make out that he had something in a box in front of him on the table. He was staring into it. I saw there was someone else further back, and before I could do anything, even speak, Ashton shouted something like, "Bloody wretch!" and there was a flash. I was blinded by it in that dark. I ran towards them. I knew gunfire in the dark when I saw it. I was groping around and grabbed hold of someone. I knew him, Rebecca. It was the Arab from the mountain, but he hadn't done it. He hadn't shot him. There was someone else there.

Our Arab ran. He was on a horse and away faster than thought. I never could keep up with him. But I went after him. I had to try. He's someone very important to me. It's not fair to you, but I can't tell you anything more. You probably suspected something and I wanted to let you know that. I couldn't—

There is then something so heavily crossed out that the page is torn. I can't make out the words.

I wanted to write to tell you that all is well and not to look for me. It wouldn't be good for you. Or for me. You won't find me where I've gone.

I'm sorry. For everything. I hope you're well. I hope you're happy.

Goodbye, Rebecca.

Robert

The pages slip from my hands onto the table. It has been years since I saw him last. Why has he written now? Why didn't he write before? He's alive! I choke back a sob.

The whole sorry affair floods back into my mind. I could almost laugh at the girl I was then, who'd thought so much of silly schemes when all she really needed to do was talk to him. The aftermath of the shooting comes before my eyes, and Robert's last flight on horseback. How I tried, hopelessly, to go after him. And that boy-officer, Avery. Anger rises in me again as I remember him. And Harpreet, with her strong, blank, beautiful, toothless face as she surrendered to that unworthy man. My tea grows cold on my desk. He is alive.

No-one ever told me what happened on that day that I saw Robert at the harbour. I was kept under guard and alone until a steamer could take me back down the coast to Bombay and onto another ship to England. As soon as I arrived home, I'd written to Horseguards to complain about my treatment, and Harpreet's, and everything that had happened in the strongest terms, but even then, I'd known it would do no good.

Living it all again so clearly, I remember the ship at Bombay. The great white side of it and its slow steam. Deep brown rust streaks in the thick iron plate. Immense noise and power enveloping me as I walked up the gangway and onboard, the world vibrating with the churn of steam and steel below. Two Indian soldiers in loose uniforms at my back.

All of this to take me away from India, from Robert; how could I resist, how could I fight against it? The gangway was withdrawn and the soldiers left, their duty done. And in spite of my better self, in spite of everything, and to my eternal shame, the tiniest feeling of relief crept into my heart at that moment, that I'd done all I could, I could not be reproached and that now I could leave the whole mess behind. I trod it down. It wasn't worthy. There, somewhere on that land, was

Robert, in who knew what peril. I wanted to hammer at my chest and scream for him, and instead I'd stood silent and watched the shore recede. But he got away, surely, I thought as I stood gripping the iron taffrail. He must have got away. He would find me.

Hardly thinking, I reach into one of my desk drawers to pull out something I haven't looked at for a long time. *The Times* of the seventeenth of September, 1932. The very paper that I picked up on my way to my flat on the day I arrived back in England. And there it is, still on the front page, just as I saw it as I ducked out of the rain into the musty newsagent's shop at the corner of Uncle's street almost three years ago:

> *Disgraced Archaeologist Dies*
>
> *We regret to report the demise of the archaeologist and retired Colonel of the Bedfordshire and Berkshire Light Cavalry, James Ashton. Col. Ashton passed his last weeks in Bombay, India, to which city he had been removed during August to receive treatment for wounds sustained whilst on expedition in northern Maharashtra, as reported previously by our India correspondent, Mr Arnold Rudger. It remains unknown by what hand Col. Ashton received his mortal injury and investigations continue.*

I skip over the description of the attack and Ashton's injuries, with its familiar words, 'infection', 'passed through his stomach', 'lack of proper medical facilities' and read on:

> *The Times can also reveal further details relating to Col. Ashton's sad fall from grace, of which it seems he was most likely unaware during his final days. Readers will recall the dramatic emergence of evidence that Col. Ashton's*

> *discovery, so widely covered, of the Mask of Maharashtra, was in fact a forgery, and we can now report that the matter has been taken beyond doubt by the testimony of an aged native goldsmith, local to the area of Col. Ashton's excavations…*

It still gives me a morsel of satisfaction to read of Ashton's shame, and a shred of regret that he apparently never learned of it. I do wonder, though, how it had affected poor Daisy, waiting for him in England, keeping his home and his dogs.

I come to myself again, and back into the office. Surfacing out of memory, I see the scrawled pages still in front of me on the desk, the room full of the smell of the coal fire in the grate.

"Ardeau! Come and look at this. What's this postmark?"

He comes through with the tea pot and takes the envelope in his free hand, holds it close to his face and peers at the mark.

"There's an 'H' I think." He stares a little longer, frowning. "No. I don't know, I'm afraid. It's too smeared."

"It's not an 'H', it's a 'T'," I say, taking the envelope back from him. I put my head on one side. "Oh, I don't know, it could be anything."

Ardeau is leaning over my shoulder, peering at the envelope.

"Shall I file it for you?" he says, reaching past me, his hand brushing mine. I flinch.

"No. No, Ardeau. Leave it with me. Thank you. I'll call if I need anything."

I'm still holding the envelope minutes later. Staring across my office. An old painting of one of the partners from the last century hangs opposite me, looking severe beneath beetling brows and very, very dead. I fold the letter carefully. Slide it gently back into its envelope and hold it to my face. Searching for a familiar scent, any sign that this is really from Robert. Truly from him. I put it carefully into a drawer, conscious already of the countless times I will look again to try to read that postmark.

Months pass in professional and domestic near-solitude. Work, home, sleeping, eating. I find myself speaking out loud to Robert sometimes, as if he were there. After I receive the letter I go to his home, in case, by some chance, he has come back. But there's no sign of him. The house he grew up in is locked and cold-looking. No-one in the pub has seen him for years. Not since before the war. I even go to the rectory and ask the vicar to write to me at once if Robert should ever return or if he should hear anything of him.

Perhaps in all the time that has passed since India, while I've done my articles and joined the law, putting all that awful business and any idea of love behind me, Robert has been somewhere here, in London, near me even. I start looking about me again on the streets. Why doesn't he want to be found? One day I see a man from behind and am sure it's him. My skin is hot in an instant; I break into a sweat. But it's not Robert. It's some other man. I cry behind a locked door.

I work longer hours. Eventually my name finds its way onto the list at the door, is defaced and repainted. I become more important to the business and better-paid. I become appreciated. But without him, what does it mean?

Magsie

"George, look, let's not get cross," I try. "I want to tell you about something from when I was young, I think it might help."

"Help with what? I can't think what sort of help I might need." His voice is getting quieter, but it's not calm anymore. I can feel my heart beating a little more quickly. But I have to carry on; I owe it to my little Elspeth.

"I just want to tell you a story about someone I knew, called Hassan. He was in love with someone, but they wouldn't let them be together, and the person he was in love with died, it was all so horrid…"

As I'm going on, and he's staring at me, my plan feels so thin and stupid. How did I think this would persuade him that what he's doing is wrong? But I have to try. "It was because of prejudice. It was… they wouldn't…"

I'm struggling for the right words and George says, "Wouldn't what?" He stands up and marches across the room, leans right into my face. "Wouldn't what, Mum?" He's still not shouting. He's not as angry as he was when he got back from the airport. It feels like he's enjoying his power over me and I find I'm leaning back into the cushions away from him, my own son. "Come on," he says, "let's have this story."

But there's a hammering on the door. Such a hammering that I think the stained-glass panes might break. George doesn't say a thing, but he turns towards the sound, still and silent. I start to say something about the door breaking, but he shushes me with a hiss. He lets the hammering go on for a moment, while I think he's composing himself, then he walks out into the hall and opens the door.

"Hello Mick," I hear.

"Georgie. You took your time. Now what the hell happened this morning?"

"Nothing, Mick. It's over. We're not doing anything."

I creep over to the door, my stockinged feet silent on the oak boards, and peep through the gap between the door and the frame. There he is, the big oaf, those small eyes looking out of his great potato head with its tufts of hair. As I watch, he reaches in through the doorway and grips George's arm. I can see that he's squeezing it.

"Georgie, you do know that your Elspeth's walking out with a black, right? The boys have seen it. Even seen him round your house. You do remember all that, right?"

"Leave it, Mick," says George, but he's not looking at him, his head's turned away.

"And today, when we were supposed to be round there, to nip it in the bud, you don't show, pal. What's that about? It makes me worry, Georgie. That you're the sort of prick that actually wants a load of brown grandkiddies. Tell me I ain't right," Mick gives a laugh, as if the very idea is absurd, "or I might think it's you that needs sorting out, as much as this darkie."

"All right, Micky. Fuck off now."

Mick stops laughing abruptly. "What's your problem, pal? You really are all for it, eh?"

"Look, Mick, it's not that simple." *No, George, I think, don't try, you can't reason with him. Get him out of here.* But within the fear at what this huge man might do is a glimmer of hope that George might not be as far gone down Mick's road as I'd thought.

Mick ignores George, carrying on with his theme. "You can't wait for it, eh? For your wee girl to marry Mohamed the fucking sheikh of... whatever." Mick's laughing again but stops abruptly and drops his voice lower. "But seriously, Georgie, if her da doesn't look after her, maybe I'll have to do it. Yeah, I could fucking take care of that Elspeth all right." I feel sick watching, George has shrunk into the door frame and Mick's leaning over him; I can see his smear of a mouth working as he talks, imagine the stink of the cigars that I remember he smokes because he thinks it makes him look rich.

"I'll take care of them both, Georgie," he's almost whispering now. "Take care of that Paki then take care of your... little... girl. How'd you like that you..." Mick loses the thread of his sentence and before he can pick it up again, George stands up a little taller in the doorway, cutting him off.

"I said fuck off, Mick." He almost shouts it, trying to shove Mick's bulk out of the way, to get him out of the doorway and away. But almost without pausing, the smile gone from his face, Mick swings his bulk forward and punches George in the middle of the face. I hear a crack that I think must be my son's nose breaking and George staggers back into the doorway and falls through it, with an aerial trail of blood arcing after him. I don't know how I do it, I haven't moved so fast in years, but I'm behind George before he hits the ground; I can't catch him, but I manage to scooch my handbag under his head to stop it cracking on the stone floor. Oh, my George, my little boy, I can't bear the blood and the shock on his face.

I hear Mick laughing again, and saying something that sounds like, 'fucking fairy'. He steps through the doorway into the hall. "Let's see to you, shall we, Georgie?"

He can't bend down to hit George again, he's too fat, but he lifts his great foot and stamps on George's hand. I'm too appalled at the sight even to scream. That hand I've known since the first day of his life, the fingers that were so soft and small, now beneath the hard and filthy sole of this man's brown boot. It's too much to bear. He lifts his foot again. I can't have it, won't have it. From where I sit behind my boy on the floor, I swing my stick round, hooked handle first, and get it round Mick's ankle. He's lifted his foot even higher this time and is trying to find his balance, arms outstretched, when I catch him. It's amazing that it really takes so little effort just to tip him over. All that bulky, bully man, knocked down by an old lady. He falls hard and as he does, his head hits the edge of the front door that was still open behind him with a muted thump. His head leaves a scrap of hair and blood behind. On the floor, he lies motionless for a moment, while George stares at what I've done, then Mick starts making a wheezing sound that slowly, slowly, forms itself into words that sound something like, "Fffffffuck… Ahhh… help, help me."

Still sitting on the floor, I cradle George's head in my hands and only then do I realise that behind Mick are two other men. They must have come with him and have been watching the show. Perhaps they'd also been planning to go and do whatever awful thing they were going to do to Aban. But now they only look startled. I brace myself for them to burst in and pick up where Mick had left off but, no, they look from him, burbling on the floor, to me, to George and seem nonplussed. I don't know if it's that their leader has been felled by a little old lady, or that they're shamed by the sight of me holding my poor son, but whatever it is, eventually they step quietly into the house and half-carry, half-drag Mick away. I'm a little relieved to see that once outside he revives a little and is able to walk through the gate, with one arm round each of their shoulders. Just in time for the police car to pull into view, that Jenny said she'd send past the house later to check that everything looked OK. The policemen step out straightaway and it doesn't take them long to figure out what's happened, arrest Mick, who they seem to know very well already, and have him carted away in an ambulance.

That was a defeat that he won't forget too quickly, I think. And I hope it will be enough to keep him away and, from what I've learned about Mick over the years, I think it will. I can already imagine the two disciples that were waiting outside turning from concerned to amused as soon as Mick was out of sight, and then the rumours spreading around the pub.

Rebecca

Some time after Robert's letter arrived, a major case comes in that keeps me busy for several months. A spinster has died, leaving hundreds of thousands in investments and cash, not to mention a very valuable house in west London and a cottage in Shropshire. She left the entire estate to the Royal Society for the Prevention and Cure of Pulmonary Illness – a long-standing client of the firm, and of which one of our partners, Sir Robby Elfstead, is chairman – but the bequest has been challenged by her daughter. Waiting to discuss the case with Sir Robby, who is away on other business, I find myself with a free afternoon, so I pull out the letter again and stare at the envelope. *Surely there must be something*, I think, as if by simply willing it I can make the postmark become clear. I turn it over in the light of my window. Nothing. Bitterly, I throw the envelope and pages onto my desk and they skim across the smooth leather top and flutter away, the sheets settling face down on the floor.

But something on the paper has me dashing round my desk to reach it, clattering my chair into the wall as I go. How could I have missed it? In faint letters, on the reverse of the notepaper Robert has written on, is a faded grey printed heading. I strain to read it: Mr & Mrs E. Soole, Horsden House, Crafford, Devon. Robert must not have known it was there – must have picked up the paper from a pile and thought it was blank. Maybe he wasn't quite himself when he wrote the letter and didn't notice. I look again at the writing. It's crabbed and wild. Could it be stress, or fatigue, or is he ill? I read the letter for the hundredth time.

Robert says he knew the Arab. Somehow. But whether he means he knew him already, before India, or that while I was recovering he'd made his acquaintance, I don't know. But, why did he say, "I never could keep up with him?" I know I'll never get the answer by turning it over and over in my head. I have to get to Devon.

"Ardeau," I call, pulling my spectacles off. "Get me on a train to Devon! Somewhere called Crafford. I don't know if there's a branch line or... Do it, will you?"

Ardeau puts his head round the door. "Certainly. When would you like to go? Is everything well?"

"Now," I say, ignoring his other question. Of course, there's no certainty that Robert is at Horsden House. Or that he's ever been there, for that matter. He could have got the paper from anywhere. But I simply must try.

The next morning I make me way to Waterloo. Ardeau, I think, feeling slightly worried, convinced me last night that, as it was already late in the day, a morning journey might be better, when I'd had a night's sleep and some food. I certainly ate, but there was little chance of sleep. I threw off the eiderdown, put it on again, opened the window. Turned the pillow endlessly, desperate for the night to pass. I shouted into the sheets. Each hour might mean that Robert could be an hour further away and I can't lose him again now that I have this chance. But even as my hope mounts, it tumbles again, as I remember what a slender clue I have. And the months that have passed since he wrote that letter. How could I not have noticed the letterhead sooner? I curse myself for being an unforgivable, half-witted dolt.

When at last morning came, getting up, dressing and boarding the 910 bus to start my journey all made me feel a little better. At least I was taking some sort of action. And now the grand entrance to Waterloo, sooty and streaked with rain, feels like the opening to another world, one in which Robert still lives, and I surge with hopefulness again. I have many hours of journey ahead of me, through the wilding countryside to Axminster, a branch line to Benscombe, then whatever means I can find to reach Crafford. Ardeau promised to telephone ahead to make arrangements, but despite his resourcefulness, I have doubts about reaching Horsden House today, much as I wish to.

I reach Axminster in a hard rain and a strange, yellow light, the Victorian station building drab and cold, its grimy windows like clouded eyes. Few people are around and I have an hour to wait for my connecting service. I try to read the book I've brought with me, a turgid Russian novel, but I can't focus on the words or endless characters with their hundreds of names. Checking the clock I don't know how many times, I will the train to steam into view so I can continue on my way. What will he say when I arrive? Will he be angry? Livid, I think, if I know him at all. But then, when he calms down… I laugh a wild sort of laugh. But I'm getting ahead of myself again. He may not even be there.

A porter shuffles onto the platform in loose trousers and clumping shoes. He glances my way and disappears back into the ticket office. A few minutes later I hear my train coming down the line. I don't see it until it's nearly at the platform, so murky is the weather. It pulls in and belches steam across the platforms, its cheerful red paint jarring painfully with the bleak surroundings.

Inside, I find an unoccupied compartment and slide the door closed with a clunk. In the wood and leather refuge from the weather, and in a soft and comfortable seat, my mind strays back to India, my thoughts ungovernable and whirring around like a broken motor. I remember the men; Singh's blood flowing out in a glossy red sheet over his honey coloured skin.

The beatings were Ashton's undoing in the end. I didn't find out what happened to Robert after his flight from Ashkara, or to the mysterious man on the mountain, but finally the truth came out about Ashton's shooting, at least. It was much later, when I was long back in England, that Erica wrote to tell me. It wasn't one of the men whom Ashton had actually thrashed who had taken revenge but a brother. The younger boy had been maybe thirteen or fourteen, excited to be working the excavation with the great white Colonel. He'd been full of talk about it with his family at home. The elder had always been protective, ever since the younger had nearly died from dysentery when he was a child and then, when Ashton took that vile crop to him, cutting the boy's legs awfully, it was more than he could bear. He was the incredible shot – who'd taken the peacock at such range – and he still had the old muzzleloader. He waited for his chance and got into Ashton's lodgings after dark. The family who lived there were suspected of letting him in, after months of Ashton treating them as slaves, but nothing could be proved against them. The man shot Ashton at close range. He would barely have needed to aim, that time. Deliberately shot him where it would cause a slow death, they thought. When they caught him, he told the whole story and claimed the killing was revenge against Ashton for what he'd done to the boy and against the British King for his ongoing slow rape of India. He was hanged. I still think, sometimes, about the poor younger boy. What his brother's sacrifice must have meant to him. What it can have done to him.

As I sit in my carriage, I wonder if Ashton would have been more sorry about what came to light afterwards than about his own suffering and death. The truth about his grand excavation, the newspaper sensation. The murdered Colonel, the great archaeologist who turned out to have forged his greatest find. He'd had a hand-picked team of diggers with poor English and few friends, including the young boy whose beating eventually led to the murder. Ashton had them create a false site away from the main trenches. All it needed was a deep hole and some old stones from the harbour to form a cyst. The beatings were partly to drive them to faster work and partly, I think, to terrorise the men, so they wouldn't let slip the secret.

I stare out at the fields and woods marching past as my breath steams up the window in my compartment, thinking of one of the last times I saw Robert. He'd insulted me for my clumsiness, when I fell, out on our hunt. I don't remember him being overly concerned with my injury; he was so distracted. I wanted to ask him why, but I was in pain and, even then, feeling a little tired of his moods. If he wouldn't talk to me then my sympathy had its limits; I couldn't guess what was in his mind. If I'd only known I might never see him again…

Rain veins the window as the train rumbles on through the gloom. After what feels like an age, we come to my stop and I pray that Ardeau has managed some form of onward transport. Otherwise it will mean trying to find an inn.

When I step down from the warmth of the train onto a stone platform, bent trees are all around. The rain has stopped, but everything is sodden and dripping. I walk past the small station buildings and out onto the road. It's empty in either direction. In fact, I can see nothing, not even any other buildings, and the road is bounded by high hedges. A tide of frustration threatens to overwhelm me – why did I rush down here without making proper arrangements? Now here I am without even a map, so close to where Robert might be, but with no way of finding him. I sink down onto a bench beneath the station canopy, cheerless hanging baskets on either side, and begin to steel myself for walking along the road in one direction and then the other, if I have to, until I find someone. Surely there must be a village, and it must have a public house. I have sat for a minute or so and am in the act of pulling myself together and setting off when a grey pony comes into view, pulling a light trap and a man in a pork pie hat and grey beard. I can't see his eyes, which are sunk in deep sockets. He comes on at a lazy pace and when he draws level with me, stops.

"Where you for, then?" he asks, in a soft Devon burr. It takes me a moment to understand what he means.

"I'd like to find an inn. Or somewhere to stay, anyway. Is there anywhere nearby?"

"That there be. Jim's a room at the Cricketer's begging. Shouldn't wonder you could stop there." I interpret this as good news.

"Is it far?"

He raises one of his low brows at me and an eye appears, blue and steady. He appraises me for a while. "Half a mile. You can get up on the wagon."

"Are you sure? That's very kind of you." He jerks his head towards the trap and, feeling my energy rising again, I climb up.

"Who you to see, then?" he asks, as we move away.

I take a chance. "Mr and Mrs Soole. Do you know them?"

"At Crafford? I knows the house. Other side of Bearton."

"Do you know how I might get there?"

He's silent for a few moments, then says slowly, "I'm going to Crafford. Dropped off a bit of mendin' 'ere, then I take myself 'ome. You can stop in the wagon if you like. You'll have to walk back to the Cricketer's after, mind."

I thank him warmly. At this rate we'll be an hour getting to Horsden House, but I have to try. And to hope that someone is there to receive me when I arrive. I dread the thought of finding an empty house, or a bewildered Soole family and no Robert.

"Yup. It were a bit o' mendin' I done for Jim's brother. On a chest. Norm'ly I do more bigger stuff, barns and framin' and the like, but I like a little fine work sometime."

Goodness, what's he saying, try to focus. "You're a carpenter?" He is, and tells me much of his life as we wind our way, though never his name. Eventually, we draw up at the end of a driveway cut through a laurel hedge. I thank him again and try to pay him for his trouble, but he insists he was going this way anyway and needs no money. It was enough payment 'to sit and yarr a while'. He then whips up and disappears from view. Silence settles in again when the pony's slow hoof beats have faded away and I can hear my heart pounding. A cinder driveway swings away to the right where I can see the gable of a house through the trees. You've come this far, Rebecca, now start walking. But I see Robert's words again, specifically telling me not to look for him. Why would he say that? He must know I would do anything to see him again. Well, whatever it is, I'm here. And I'm going into that house.

It's clearly of a great age. Timber-framed and large and evidently built in different phases over many years; the walls and roofs are crammed together in an odd jumble. All the same, it has a sort of grandeur to it. After a time I find, amongst the bays and buttresses, a black oak front door, with an iron bell pull to one side. It's almost dark now but a faint light glistens on a tiled floor I can see through a small leaded pane. Amid the smell of wet grass and undergrowth, I reach for the bell.

Magsie

"Mum," George says, sitting up now and holding a wad of tissue to his nose, "I don't know… Thank you." You can tell it isn't easy for him but that he means it. He stands up and gives me a cuddle and it feels wonderful; I don't even mind that he gets blood all down the front of my blouse.

"Why don't you go and get yourself cleaned up, George? I'll tidy up a bit down here."

He nods and starts off toward the stairs but turns, with one hand on the walnut newel post. "Mum, I'm sorry I haven't come down much. It's only since Dad went… I can't…"

"It's all right," I say; I don't want him to have to put it into words. I touch his poor hand and he winces slightly. He seems to have deflated somehow, since I arrived, all that beetrootness has fallen away. "I miss him too," I say, "every day." But as I say it, I realise that, somehow, I've shed something too. I've hardly thought of Simon since I took off from London. He's always there at home, sitting in every chair, waiting for me in bed, but here, away and out in the world, I'm not just half of what used to be 'us'. I'm me.

George goes off up the stairs. He trudges, head down, and sighs as he turns out of sight at the top. He'll feel better in a while, I'm sure of it. He'll never see Mick again, there's no need to, this is a big city, and he'll move on with his life. With his family. Another key in the door breaks my train of thought.

"My God, Magsie, what is it this time?"

It's Nastia, looking appalled at the mess of her immaculate hallway and the blood covering my blouse.

"It's nothing, nothing, don't worry, I was tidying up."

"But what…?"

"Oh, that's George's," I say, and her hand flies up to her face.

"No, no, don't worry, it's only his nose. Nothing awful. It was that Mick, but don't worry, he's all sorted out now. We sent him packing." I enjoy telling her the story of felling the beast as I make her a cup of tea. I think I'm going to enjoy telling it a few more times, too.

Rebecca

Gripping the iron handle, I pause before announcing myself with the clamour of bells. I feel so alert, as if prepared for danger, with the cold metal in my hand and rough brickwork behind my knuckles. I take a deep breath and turn away, close my eyes for a moment. I can smell the grass. It's been cut recently, probably one of the last cuts of the year. Clippings scatter the edges of the brick path where I stand. The flower beds to either side are carefully kept. To my left is a copse of young trees, fenced against the deer. I see squirrel traps attached to some of the slender trunks, a bushy tail hanging down from one. There is no movement. Turning back to the door, I pull the handle.

I wait for what feels like a long time and pull again. The faint glow is still reflected on the red tiled floor beyond the glass, but no-one comes, so I knock; I can't leave. I have to know if he's here, or if he's been here. Then, I find that I'm turning an iron knob and pushing open the heavy front door.

Unlocked, it swings inward noiselessly. I step onto the red tiles and start in shock as a scaly eye fixes on me. A huge, grey parrot in a cage, pink about the eyes and with a black bill and claws. It gives what sounds like a cough – an old woman's stifled hacking – and I wonder who the bird is aping, whether they are alive or dead. It grips the bars of the cage with its beak and, with its great talons below, climbs to the top of its tall iron home, never releasing me from its stare. I edge past it on the other side of the hallway and find myself in an inner hall of whitewashed daub walls with dark stained doors leading from it. I start to call out, but my voice falters and I say nothing. There's a gentle, slow sound of a clock and I follow it. A black metal latch on the door to my left opens with a loud crack as I press on the thumb plate and for a moment I stand still as death. But nothing follows the sound, save the ever-onward ticking. Inside I find a drawing room, a great dark rug with a heavy floral design. It's tidy and, unlike the hall which has a musty smell, this room is scented with polish. There's a fireplace with three wooden armchairs, two to the far side and one nearest me, and next to an open hearth with black firedogs are two garish porcelain creatures with black eyes; I suppose they are meant to be canine, but the result is monstrous. The grate is cold ash.

On the far side of the room between two windows opening to the front of the house is a rolltop desk. I try the handle and the top slides up quietly; it seems well-used. Within is a stack of paper headed in the same faded grey font and envelopes to match. I feel a surge in my stomach. Running my hand over the desktop and its rich patina of years, I wonder if Robert has sat here. Sliding the desk top closed again, I turn back towards the door. There seems little point in staying, there being no-one around, and I have to find the Cricketer's Arms before it gets much later.

But as my fingers touch the latch, I hear heavy boot-steps coming from further back in the depths of the house. A man's voice singing quietly. Robert? Could it be? Still and silent, I strain to hear, to recognise his voice or something familiar in the movements. Holding my breath, I open the latch as gently as I can, and manage it without a sound. My shoes are soft brogues with only a small heel and, walking carefully, I negotiate the tiled hallway silently, moving towards the noise. It grows louder. I hear him put something heavy down, perhaps on a kitchen table. He's talking with a cheerful voice, to a dog? At least, no-one is responding. If I can get a little closer, I'll be able to tell if it's him for certain. A door in front of me, at the end of the hall, has a round brass knob instead of the black latches of the other doors. I reach out and, ever so slowly, begin to turn it.

"Who are you, then?" A voice from behind hits me like an electrical shock; I leap and scream, spinning round to see who's there. It's a girl, standing near the parrot's cage. She must have come from one of the other doorways off the hall. How did I not hear her? She's real enough, with wavy brown hair and a loose white dress with a lace collar, feet in thick knitted socks. We stare at each other for a moment, then the door with the brass knob bursts open and there stands a huge man carrying a shotgun, pointing at my chest. He's shouting something as he comes through the door, but when he sees me, he stops with a stunned expression. I think a smartly dressed woman in spectacles is not what he expected to see and, from the way he looks at them, I'm pretty sure that he's never seen anyone but a man wearing trousers before this moment.

Taking advantage of his momentary confusion, I say, "Rebecca Hellings. Elfstead and Co Solicitors."

He shakes my hand with a slightly dazed look. "John Soole. Um… This is my house. And farm." He looks at the girl, whom I take to be his daughter, as if for assistance, but she has withdrawn a little behind the parrot's cage. I say hello to her too and she comes towards me.

"This is Magsie," says Mr Soole. "She's not been well, she's… minding the house… but," he seems to collect himself a little, "what are you doing here?" He breaks the shotgun and places it in a corner (I notice it's not loaded). Now that we're talking, I drop my official tone and take a step towards him.

"I hope you can help me, Mr Soole. I'm looking for someone."

"In trouble, is he?"

"No. No, he's a friend. I think… I think he might have been staying here."

"Hassan, you mean?" he asks, and turns to Magsie. "Magsie, run out to the barn, will you?"

"Hassan? No, I'm looking for a man called Robert. Robert Baker."

Mr Soole's face clouds and he looks down.

"Ah, Robert. I wondered if anyone would come."

"So you do know him?" I ask, taking another step forward and reaching out with my hands to take Mr Soole's in my own. He's still looking away and frowning now. "Please. Please. Is he here? Where is he? Please tell me." My throat closes. "Please."

Mr Soole doesn't move away. He keeps his hands in mine and is silent for a long time.

"I'm sorry," he says eventually, and, with a voice that cracks, "he's dead."

And then, there he is, the man from the mountain, the Arab, walking out from the barn when I run from the house and this farmer with his vile news. I stagger and almost fall as the man turns to look at me, pausing as he rubs his head with a scrap of towel. He must have done it, how else could Robert have been here but be dead? Even as I hear Mr Soole coming out after me through the door, I fly at this man who's taken my Robert from me, hurling my bag at his head. He dodges it, then I'm on him, beating and kicking him wherever I can. He falls down and I try to strike at his face, but he throws me off, so I grab the wooden pail he's been using to wash with, still half full of water, and make to swing it at his head.

He'd have been out cold, maybe killed, I'm sure of it, but Mr Soole takes hold of me and tears the bucket from my hands before it can find its mark. The Arab stares, shocked, blood on his mouth, and Mr Soole is shouting, shouting, and I am screaming as the farmer holds me, "You killed him! You killed him! You killed my Robert!" and it only comes to me slowly, through the pain and anger and loss, that the man, too, is crying. On his knees, he's weeping like a child, sobs tearing out of him and his face a mask. I catch myself, try to think… this is the man, I know it. But what is he saying? I can't hear, and cry at Mr Soole to release me.

"I'm sorry, Miss, I can't do that," he says. "You looked fit to kill him a minute ago. I don't know what it is you think happened with your Robert but…"

The Arab stands and wipes his eyes, reaches out to take my hand. I flinch away, but he says, so gently, "He wasn't your Robert. He was mine."

Robert

India, 1932

Robert can scarcely remember how he caught up with him. Where the days have gone since the shooting. The man in the dark. The blood that he'd heard, more than seen, running from Ashton's wound. A man's life pouring out onto the floor.

But now, here he is, after all this time. All the wasted time. He'd never dreamed that he'd see him again. Never outside the quiet imaginings that Robert sometimes let himself have when alone and behind closed doors. Anything else has been too dangerous. Too much for his peace of mind to bear.

There have been others, of course, secretly, privately. Rebecca helped him to hide, not that she knew. A chap who'd caught his eye at cricket and lingered in the pavilion after the others had left. Matthew, whom he'd almost loved, but whose terror of his mother and father's disappointment meant such anxious secrecy that it could never be.

But no-one had been like Hassan, no-one had been close. And now here he is, sweating, real. Standing with his horse amid the stink and shouts of the harbour, men and women, children, dogs. He is here. The weight of it seems to crush Robert's chest. No breath will come.

When he saw him on the mountain, he thought it had been some fantasy, some mirage of yearning. He couldn't believe it was him, then, couldn't bear to. In case he was wrong. In case a hope was reawakened but proved false. He couldn't have lived through that, he knew. It would be the end. But he felt more sure as time went by, as he played back in his mind again and again the vision of the man at the ridgeline, as he looked down at them, as he turned away, silhouetted against the brilliant blue sky. He'd tried to find him, tried to run after him, but had never caught up until now. And here – here in front of him – he is. Hassan. The one who's been apart from him for so many years, but with him every day.

Hassan is speaking. What does he say? Robert fights to focus.

"I didn't... it wasn't... that man. I not shoot him." Finally, the chest opens, the air rushes in. Robert starts to laugh. He laughs for the longest time, tears running down his cheeks, until he's gasping again. He goes to hug Hassan but at the last moment holds back, instead gripping his arm – too tightly.

"I know it wasn't you, you dolt," he says, gathering himself. "D'you think I don't know you at all? We have met, you know, once or twice."

"I worked for that man," says Hassan. "I was... meant to keep secret but watch the men, keep an eye. He was paying me when... it happened."

Hassan shakes his head, looking down at the ground, and Robert squeezes his arm again, then looks around them.

"Hassan, we need to go somewhere… a bit more… They may be looking out for us. I've probably been a bit foolish coming after you but, well it's done now. And I don't regret it, come what may." Robert tries to pull Hassan away from the open space at the wharves, but Hassan stands still, his face a mask of worry.

"I didn't…" he hesitates, finding the words, "I couldn't come. You understand? To you. It wouldn't have been good. With that Ashton. It would have been not good for you or me. He was dangerous."

Robert stands close and looks him in the face. "You think any of that counts for anything now? Come on." Robert takes the horse and, as they walk away, gently holds the spot on the reins that Hassan's touch has darkened, watches Hassan's strong back as it moves beneath his *kurta pyjama*, sees the movement of his dark hair. He can remember its smell like it was yesterday, its faint mustiness, of course he can; they were the only days that mattered in his life. He breathes in deeply and closes his eyes. Now he is himself again. The veil has fallen. At last.

But they can't risk staying openly in the town, Robert knows. Ashkara is a small place and poor and they would stand out. So they walk out and up into the hills to where the landscape is clearer of trees, the sea opening up wide behind them as they climb. Talk comes slowly at first but then bursts like a dam and they are lost in it, hardly aware of the land and heat and sky around them. They talk through the day and into the night, talk as they swim in a lake they come upon, tucked into a green valley far above the sea and, later, talk as they cook fish over an open fire. When they sleep it's under the sky.

Hassan rides out at dawn, telling Robert he'll find them some supplies. He'll be careful, he says, don't worry, he's used to keeping himself hidden. He goes bare-headed, leaving his rifle with Robert. But before he mounts to head down the mountain, Robert clings to him and won't let go; a man swimming in cool water after years in burning sands.

When Hassan leaves, Robert lies on the hard ground, reliving that moment and their night before. Here is the start of their lives. Now. All they have to do is get away from India, get Hassan away, to the place they've always talked about. The place they can live quietly and alone. They'll need to be careful for a little while, then, life.

When Hassan returns, he's been riding hard, his horse is foaming and slick with sweat beneath him. He leaps from the saddle, dropping *roti* and fruit.

"Robert. Woman you were with – who is she?"

"What? Why? What's happened?"

"She's your friend?"

"Yes. Yes, my friend. Hassan, what's happened?"

"She's in danger."

"Damn it, Rebecca, what have you done? What is it, Hassan?" Hassan rushes out the story and Robert has to slow him down, calm him a little before he understands.

"So you heard this boy telling the garrison commander about a woman fugitive? A white woman? How do you know it was her?"

"How many other white women around here? The boy said this one dressed like a man."

"Well, that sounds like her, right enough. Hang it all, what the devil is she playing at?" But to Robert it's quite clear. She must have come after him. She always has, even when he'd been wretched to her, which was more often than he cares to remember. He swears and rubs at his hair. The he drops his hands and looks at Hassan.

"I have to help her."

Rebecca

Devon, 1935

WAS THERE EVER A GREATER FOOL THAN ME? I think, as I look at this man, Hassan. Small wonder that Robert warned me off coming. He would have known what this would do to me, all along he knew how I felt, he must have done. But I only realise how big a fool I am, what I've really done to them, when Hassan tells me. Before that, part of me still wants to thrash Hassan again for his part in the deceit, the cruel hiding, the secrecy, that allowed me to go on hoping and searching, believing that one day could be Robert's and mine together and for the rest of our lives. But I look at him again, how broken he is, the hollowness in his face. And the worst comes.

"He was wounded," says Hassan, and he pauses for a long time before saying, "when he came back for you."

"What do you mean, came back for me?"

"I'm sorry," he says, struggling to get the words out, "I didn't mean to… I wouldn't have say anything but… Robert had got away. He found me and we… they…" He swallows. "They shot him… through the side as he was… trying to get away."

"But," I say, "he got back here, how did he get back?"

Hassan is silent again for a while, looking at the floor, then seems able to carry on, "They didn't kill him, not for a long time. That…" he closes his eyes, "that man Avery had him locked up in the fort, even with his wound, no medical treatment, no doctors." I struggle even to ask about the conditions but Hassan leaves nothing of the filth and squalor to the imagination. Poor, poor Robert. "We'd agreed this is where we'd meet, if he got out, we thought this was our best chance, somewhere we could live quietly and in private. And he was released, once they caught the real killer, but it was too late. Avery had done for him, locking him up with that wound. We didn't ever knew what was, the infection, no doctor knew, but it killed him, my Robert."

Hassan covers his face with his hands and, slowly, I understand what this means and it's more than I can bear. Robert had got away, he'd got to his love, they were going to make it, going to have their life together. And I went blundering through the forest after them, chasing them down until at last I brought Avery's bullet all the way to his beautiful skin and killed him. With a ragged cry, I fall back against Mr Soole, who holds onto me with his rough hands and tells me it's not my fault. But it is. It is.

Perhaps one day I'll forgive myself, and forgive Robert, understand that he hadn't any choice but to hide. But that forgiveness feels as far out of reach now as Robert is. Instead I put my hands out to Hassan, take his sleeve and pull him close into my arms. I know that now, after everything, I will live with Robert forever.

Magsie

I don't think Elspeth understands why George apologises to her so much that night, through his tears. She doesn't know how close he came this morning to doing something so dreadful. Nastia doesn't either. But he does and I do, and we'll never forget it. In the end, as he holds on to his daughter, I realise I didn't need to tell him my story. But it was Hassan and Robert who made me tear up the country and remind him what family's for. They saved my Elspeth.

And I know I shan't go back to that house. I don't need to live in the past anymore. "Elspeth," I say the next morning at breakfast, "could you help me book a flight?"

"Of course, Granny," she says, "back to Gatwick?"

"No," I say, "to India."